Assimilation

Tales of transformation and surrender

First Edition

Published by The Nazca Plains Corporation
Las Vegas, Nevada
2012

ISBN: 978-1-61098-239-9
E-Book ISBN: 978-1-61098-240-5

The author hereby asserts his copyright throughout the world for the manuscript, *Assimilation*.

Published by

The Nazca Plains Corporation ®
4640 Paradise Rd, Suite 141
Las Vegas NV 89109-8000

PUBLISHER'S NOTE
Assimilation is a work of fiction created wholly by bootbrush's imagination. All characters are fictional and any resemblance to any persons living or deceased is purely by accident. No portion of this book reflects any real person or events.

Author's Photo, Chris Chan
All Other Photos and Illustrations, bootbrush

Art Director, Blake Stephens

Assimilation

Tales of transformation and surrender

First Edition

bootbrush

Dedication

To Geoff: my lover, partner, mentor and soul-mate.

Thank you for rattling my cage and setting me free;
without you, I am nothing – with you, I can be anything.

And to Nigel: the Man I am PROUD to call Master and friend.

Thank You for showing me why we call it 'play',
and for helping to me find the TRUE pup inside myself.

It is an honour to know and love you both:
my beautiful, wonderful Men.

Acknowledgements

My thanks must first go to Geoff: for being the best editor and contributor I could ever wish for (not to mention patiently enduring my obsessions with wit and good grace for so long).
I swear that we'll get to catch up on the digi-box soon!

HUGE hugs go to Shaz: for doing a brilliant job of editing (despite not being the 'target audience'). Thank you for donning your 'grammar fanatic hat', and needling me over my random capitalisation and un-closed subordinate clauses.
I owe you an afternoon in the chocolatier of your choice…

Special thanks also go to Bob, Dan and Loki:
for proof reading and giving your thoughts on the work-in-progress.

And of course, special thanks to Doug:
for encouraging his 'guru-pup' to publish in the first place.

My thanks must also go to the many guys who have helped to inspire both my sexual identity and my fiction across the years: to Adam, Simon and Derek – Robert and Denny, Bill and David – Martin, Steve and Coen – Lthredge, Lthrhypno, Robear and Salfordskin –

– and not forgetting all the guys at EMC/FUKC, the Backstreet, Hoist, and Gear –

and the whole amazing community of pups on pupzone – My thanks also to both Invincible and Wet-Hot Rubber – for keeping me supplied with beautifully made gear for all these years.

And of course – my love, devotion and thanks go to Nigel: without whom I would not be the blissfully happy puppy that I am today!

And finally: my thanks go to you, my reader: for letting me into your head and for sharing my fantasies. I hope that this will be only the first of many visits.

Namaste!

Table of Contents

Balls to bone – and everything in between.

About these stories…

Transformation, perversity, surrender, and submission. The stories in this anthology feature many of the same themes – and most of them are wrapped within a dark, glossily hypnotic skin of rubber…

They take inspiration from '*Assimilation*': one of my earliest attempts at erotic fantasy. It is a tale of absorption by living rubber, of a slow conversion into a sexualised rubber object, eager only to love and serve my transformer – and the intense pleasure that this transformation creates within me. I thought that I was unique in having this fantasy, but these themes seem to resonate with many of my rubber brethren – who say that they feel the same desire for a metamorphosis that will free them from the limitations that humanity and society place upon us.

Because, rubber really *does* seem to have a unique power out of all the gear fetishes. To those of us who have yielded to its siren song, a pure skin of rubber is the gateway into another world of masculinity and hunger, transformation and freedom. It glosses us over in anonymity and arousal, and in doing so empowers our desires and deepens our hunger – enabling us to test and push and explore at the very limits of experience and play.

In rubber, we all become one brotherhood in perversity.

But there are also other fetishes described here: bondage, hypnosis, pup-play, water-sports... Perhaps it is a personal selection of fetishes and fantasies, confessions and obsessions, but I still hope that you may find both arousal and inspiration amongst them. If you read closely, you might even be able to trace a thread of personal growth and self-awareness within them: a small history of one pervert's journey from a lonely and guiltily obsessed boy, fantasising about kidnap and abuse, to a man who now embraces his desires playfully, and found both love and fulfilment in doing so.

Finally – whilst all of these stories are the product of my own fevered brain, many of them where inspired by personal experience, and by conversations and interactions with many sexy and beautifully perverse Men over the years. I may not be able to give your real names, but my sincere thanks go to you all for helping me to become the very happy pervert that I am today.

PLEASE NOTE: *All of these tales are works of fiction – even those that are written in the first person. Many feature extreme and potentially dangerous play. The inclusion of these acts is neither a vindication of them, nor a suggestion that they should ever be attempted in real life.*

Enjoy – but remember that these are works of fantasy and fiction – nothing more.

Play safe, play responsibly – and live to play again.

bootbrush, 2012

*"…I am mutating into something other than
I was: I am becoming rubber…"*

Assimilation

Rubber is strong.

Rubber enfolds, entices and entrances.

Rubber imprisons, governs and controls.

Rubber alters perverts and transforms.

––––––––––

I am mutating into something other than I was: I am becoming rubber.

Rubber coats my body, penetrates it, flows across and through it. Rubber ripples across my skin and pumps through my blood. Rubber worms its way into my ears, my nose, my mouth and arse. It oozes between my fingers, drips down my throat, seeps between the gaps in my bones and swirls around the cavity of my skull. Rubber moves through me until every cell is coated, every nerve insulated, every part of me rubberised and assimilated.

The process is slow, purposeful, unrelenting, and irreversible – and it feels like slowly drowning in a rising black tide of ecstasy.

At first I could see myself reflected in the mirrors hung above the table where I am restrained – could see as my body and identity were taken from me under the rising tide of rubber. With fascinated horror and ghoulish arousal I watched as the rubber coated every part of me, smoothed out every crease and wrinkle, bump and curve. I watched, helpless, as the rubber rippled over my limbs, reducing them to mere glossy approximations of themselves – watched my feet change to toe-less mounds, my hands become smooth and glove-like – and saw my shaved scalp fading into glossy black as the rubber flowed up my neck and over my head, transforming it into a seamless rubbery ball.

And now, finally – wide-eyed and panting in fear and excitement – I feel the rubber pooling into the hollow of my eyes as they turn blank, glossy and empty…

As my vision fades into blackness, the last image seared into my mind is of my body assimilated and unrecognisable: every sign of humanity smoothed away beneath the thickening layers of rippling rubber skin. I am left with the image of myself become the mere impression of a man – and, gods help me, I am wracked with a shudder of pure perverted pleasure at this total surrender to rubberisation.

I feel the rubber flow over me in the blind darkness: it seeps through my parted lips, coats my teeth and tongue, fills my mouth and slides down my throat. Tireless and irresistible it pumps into me: fills my stomach, packs my throat – and seals my mouth with a throbbing, rippling mass.

The rubber flows, and every part of me loses definition and identity. It slips around my arse cheeks, coats and mounds them into the perfect rubbered bubble-butt. My back arches from the table as a thin rubbery tendril teases into my puckered hole. The probing intrusion slowly grows into a widening plug that fills my gut and presses hard against my aching prostate. I twist helplessly as the thin neck expands, stretching the ring of muscle painfully wide – then it smoothes itself out, and seals my hole forever.

I shudder as even my cock and balls are contained and transmuted as the rubber ripples up, warm and silky-smooth around my head and glans. I groan into the rubber gag as a thread of rubber carefully probes my piss-slit, then worms its way down inside my cock and into my bladder… My balls roil at the heat of the rubber as it flows over them – cupping and then squeezing them as it moulds them into a tight rubbery mass. I feel the rubber as it drips from the end of my cock: a thin drool of glossy black that thickens and tightens as it pulls my rubber-sealed head downwards – down to my glossy balls. The rubber pulses within me as the two bond and merge into one. I sob within the darkness as I realise that my whole crotch and manhood is pierced and restrained within seamless rubber: transmuted into a smooth ball – a rubberised prison, that makes me incapable of erection or ejaculation…

But in the shuddering pleasure of transformation I know that the rubber is preparing me for a new life. That the denial of all genital sensation will leave my whole vulcanised body tingling with an intense and perfect arousal that will never end. An arousal that will focus my newly assimilated mind upon its only true purpose and duty: the service for which I begged, was prepared for and am now being transformed to complete.

And still the rubber transformation continues.

Every nerve, every cell, trembles with ever increasing pleasure. My senses are overwhelmed by the touch, the smell, the taste of rubber flowing through every inch of my body. My brain throbs into overload as every part of me aches with the sensations that jolt through it as the rubber consumes and transmutes it.

Under that blissful onslaught, I feel my mind quiver and dissolve.

————

Once, rubber was merely one of my kinks. I was introduced to it by a friend whom I met in an online chat-room – and had my first experience of it jacking-off in a newly bought pair of rubber briefs and gloves whilst he watched me on cam and guided me to let go to its enticing warm wet embrace…

But the rubber was strong.

The intensity of that first experience subtly worked its erotic touch into my mind. I wanted the rubber more and more – gradually found that I could not get hard without the smell and the feel of it near. Slowly the rubber began to define my sexual identity, and I spent months collecting gear until I could lose myself within layers of complete skin-tight encasement…

The more I gave myself to that erotic rubber dependency, the more I found myself overwhelmed by the arousal it raised within me. I was swallowed by a slowly growing hunger to surrender and submit – to let the rubber deeper into me, into my mind. A need to let the rubber own and control me completely.

To let the rubber *become* me.

The more I surrendered to the rubber, the more this hunger grew – and the more I yearned to give. I found myself spending days alone, sealed within my layers of rubber and wrapped in a blissful fog of pleasure and arousal. I became absorbed into the breathless embrace of rubber – lost in ecstatic darkness and entranced by the whispering voices of submission and surrender.

I went online, sought out others like me: willing addicts to the rubber, slaves to its erotic pleasure. I became drunk on the images of encasement, transformation and submission that they shared. And within every community and forum, there was always that same first friend: encouraging and guiding me ever deeper into my obsession and rubber surrender…

Artfully, he had me meet him online whenever I was rubber encased and yearning for surrender. He understood my hunger, gave voice to the rubber, and the needs that were forming in my arousal-fogged mind. I found myself mesmerised by his deep and familiar voice as it purred from the speaker, and filled my head with images of blissful transformations and perfected rubber bodies.

His voice became the voice of my Rubber Master – and it was as this that He finally gave me permission to surrender to Him, and the relentless enticing pull of my hunger and need.

And so I found myself here: cleaned, shaved and prepared – drugged and entranced and stretched upon his table. Willingly surrendered to the process that will finally make me one with the rubber – and His for all time.

———

My body trembles – blind and dumb but shaking with the intensity of its transformation. Every fibre, cell, and nerve – everything consumed and transformed into the rubber that has fascinated and guided me for so long. I am overwhelmed by the intensity of the rubber invasion. My brain soaked in chemicals and dissolving into ecstasy, I shudder into surrender to the rubber that first enticed and now consumes me.

I cannot resist it. I do not *want* to resist it. With the relentless process of assimilation, the rubber finally becomes my whole world.

And now, that process nears its end as the rubber rewires and reprograms my mind – dissolves my memory and consumes what remains of my will. With every jolt of rubber-induced pleasure, I feel another layer of my old personality expand and fragment – willingly surrendered to the rubber in payment for the promise of ever-greater arousal.

And as each layer and boundary ghosts into extinction, that promise is fulfilled in a shudder of ecstatic surrender like I have never known.

I am dimly aware of losing myself. Of surrendering everything that I am, everything that I was – surrendering to *become*… Under the rising tide of ecstasy I realise I can no longer remember my name, or how I came to be here – my memory of anything before the rubber and its slow transformation fades into greyness, and I gladly let it go. Insulated from my past and all outside influences I am lost in a world of swirling black ecstasy.

I feel the rubber reach out once more. I feel it squirm deep into the core of my mind, reaching for the last dim part of what I once was – the last shred of ego, the final barrier to complete rubberisation. I feel it tease and probe deep into my mind, pulsing through into my subconscious. Under that relentless black pressure of ecstasy, I feel myself slowly opening up – let it dissolve the walls of that final refuge within.

My body convulses as I finally feel the tendril of rubber pierce through. There is a wash of welcoming pleasure, and then my mind relaxes around the thickening flow of rubber as it pumps black ecstasy into the very core of all that I am. As the dark flow takes me I feel a shudder of complete and utter surrender to that which I am becoming. Then every thought and sense fades into perfect blackness.

Now there truly is no "before", no "past", no "I".

Now there truly is only the rubber…

———

Released from its bonds, a new creature arises from the table with black fluidity.

It is no longer merely human, but a rubberised vessel: its mind perfectly empty and ready for programming. It knows only intense arousal and the need to serve.

A rubberised being, it sinks to its knees before the Master who has controlled and subtly manipulated it over many years.

A Rubber Master who recognised the perverse potential in this innocent from the first time they met online, and who has spent years in quietly guiding him to this new destiny. Befriending and then subtly encouraging, enticing and perverting: quietly implanting His own subtle suggestions of rubberised surrender under layers of talk whilst the young man was horny, vulnerable, and unaware – then gently nurturing this seed into a deep subconscious need. Bonding that need for submission to the man's growing rubber fetish, using it to deepen and expand His own Masterly control. Slowly gaining his complete trust and gently dissolving his will. Enticing and entrancing him with pleasure and deferred arousal – gradually preparing him to make the final step into complete and utter rubber slavery…

And now that innocent kneels before his Master: completely transformed by the process of rubberisation, unaware of the long journey he has made from man to machine. Transmuted physically and mentally into the perfect rubber slave. Stripped of its past and programmed only to Serve, to Love, to Obey.

The Master reaches down and strokes His rubber slave's smooth head – notes the tremble of pleasure that passes through its glossy limbs. He extends a booted foot and touches its rubber-sealed genitals. He hears its muffled moan as it responds and rises to let Him slide His boot under its smooth arse, then presses its now-useless crotch into His boot leather. It leans submissively into His leg.

The Master knows that with this rubberised castration the slave is denied all release and so is now only capable of pleasure at His hands – pleasure through serving Him. He smiles in the knowledge that it is now completely dependent upon Him and what He provides for it. He knows that, devoid of all self-awareness, it is now utterly obedient: pliant to His every whim and fantasy. Eager only to learn. To Serve. To Obey. To Please.

The Master smiles down at His new slave, absently reaches down to stroke His gloved hand over the tight arousal in His leathered crotch. He feels a thrill of pleasure by the instant reaction in His slave, as the glossy rubber smoothness of its head splits and opens to reveal an undulating tube of rubber. He knows that the slave is hungry to be fed. He knows that it will feel the rubber pulsating throughout its whole body in anticipation – that its dull mind will be awash with intense hunger and stimulation, and swamped with the need to pleasure and serve Him.

He revels in this feeling of complete possession of another being. He feels the power in knowing that this is what that the slave was created for – what He has twisted that young man to want and *need* to be.

He pauses to relish the moment – lets Himself feel the heady wash of control and domination, before performing the last act that will seal His slave's fate once and for all – and make it His forever.

Then, slowly, He places both hands on either side of the slave's completely smooth head. He feels it tip its face slightly forwards, making itself ready for Him. He can feel the slight tremble though the rubber as the creature's hunger intensifies at His touch.

He sees the rubberised tube of a throat glisten through the small opening – sees it flowing outwards towards the throbbing tip of its Master's cock. With a muffled grunt the Master slides Himself into that waiting hole. He feels the rippling ecstasy as the slave's rubberised face flows apart and then closes around Him – ripples up and over Him to caress every inch of His straining meat.

He feels it open and transform itself to fit His desire and unspoken command: feels the rubber flutter and pulse along His shaft. He shivers as the cool smoothness of the living rubber moulds around him, then shudders as it obediently melts and flows to cup His balls. It slides down the inside of His thighs to caress them in slick muscular undulations.

With a shudder of pride and ownership, He feels His rubber slave pleasuring Him like it has been programmed to do – pleasuring Him like no *man* ever could. It is a perfect rippling tube of obedient rubber that feeds on His control as it mindlessly, perfectly, obediently takes Him deep into its body. Never getting tired, never needing to stop for breath, incapable of gagging, it tirelessly pleasures Him and draws Him ever closer to the most exquisite of orgasms…

And as the Master arches His back and growls in pleasure, the slave at His feet knows only perfect ecstasy and contentment. It feels its Master's meat throb and pulse within it – feels the tremble of the rubber in its arse and throughout its whole body. It feels the waves of intense orgasm that flows from its Master and into it – reverberating and reflecting within its rubbered body to produce a pleasure beyond anything that either has ever felt.

It feels its very soul shudder as its Master pumps His seed into its hungry body – finally and completely embraces its true destiny: knows itself to be irrevocably changed and transformed into everything that the Master promised it would be:

No longer a young man now, but the Master's perfect rubber slave.

"…my body is encased beneath its shiny black covering…"

Becoming a rubberman

There is something unique about Rubber:

Its unique, faintly chemical scent makes my pulse quicken and my mind cloud.

The touch of it – warm, clinging, tight, and enclosing against my skin – makes me want things, NEED things that my ordinary self would normally shy away from (yet secretly yearn for…).

Sometimes I resist. But the suitcase under the bed calls, and the men in the pictures beckon, and soon I'm there again – dry-mouthed and sweaty palmed – as I anoint my trembling body with lube and then slowly, carefully draw on that embracing rubber skin…

As my body is encased beneath its shiny black covering and the warming rubber releases its heady aroma, I know I secretly yearn to have this other rubber self take over completely, to leave behind forever the mundane, the ordinary…

To finally become a true RUBBERMAN.

————

Although I love rimming and arse play, I have never been fucked much.

Not to say my arse has never been filled. Hell, as I write this I have the dildo of the rubber sheathed pants I am wearing filling my hole, and I'm not complaining – oh no Sir!

I'm wearing multiple rubber layers over those pants too: two pairs of latex shorts over each other, a couple of tight T-shirts – and a full one-piece catsuit sealing the whole lot in. I have a 3" collar buckled tightly around my neck.

I've set a mirror so I can see myself at the keyboard: the tight layers show off my chest, shoulders and arms; the arms make my biceps look bigger too. As I move my legs, I can see the exited bulge of my throbbing cock – even though it is strapped down under multiple layers of rubber. My hand drifts down – it feels only smooth rubber – it squeaks as I draw it over my crotch.

If I rock slightly the dildo moves in my arse – I feel a sting as the muscles clench and struggle to push out the intrusion. I rock forward, rock back. In and out, up and down. My arse begins to relax, and I feel the dildo sliding deeper into me until it rubs hard against my prostate. The resisting layers of rubber press against my sheathed cock, heightening my pleasure.

I take a hit of the poppers... first nothing – then the rush. I feel my heart's heavy pounding. The blood rushes to my face, cock and arse – it throbs past the tight collar. My head feels tight and hot – but I feel good.

As the blood pumps in my ears the noises of the world fade in and out in time...

Now is the time that I'd want you – my rubbered Master – to be here. To teach me, train me, transform me into your rubber slave: an anonymous being of only rubber, sustained by your desire and nourished by your body.

A rubber toy, a pet, a mere extension of your rubber body with no will of its own other than to please and satisfy. Contained by your rubber suit, and breathing only your amyl-filled atmosphere through its hooded gas mask…

I sense you behind me; feel the touch of your gloved hands as they reach around me to pull that hooded gas mask over my head. I feel it slide over me, slip into place with a snap. The rubber mouthpiece seats under my chin and cups my nose.

Through the glass lenses, I see you screw in the canister. The poppers seep into the mask – swirl round my face, slide up my nose and down my throat. They surround and fill me and I'm momentarily disoriented by the hot, hungry blood that courses through me.

You push me backwards and I feel my legs hit a surface; I sit back and find myself on a rubber covered bed. With relief, I see you reach for the poppers again – the connecting tube swings as the canister is refilled, then I feel my skin expand to fill the suit. I begin to sweat. My hands wander across my body and I can't help moaning in excitement as they find only tight, stretched rubber. Not an inch of my old skin exists anymore.

I take another hit of the poppers. My cock swells. I'm on the way to transcending human. I'm on my way to becoming a being of only rubber.

I feel you touch my inner thighs as you move to kneel between them. I move my legs apart to let you closer, deeper. My hand reaches for the rubber of your hooded head. I see my sheathed cock disappear through the hole in your mask. With a shudder, I fall back onto the sheets.

There is a sensation of cold at my arse as you open the zip – then all I can do is twitch and moan as the dildo slides out, to be replaced by a hot, hungry tongue. I put my feet onto the edge of the bed, spread my legs, and slowly pull my arse cheeks apart. Your tongue probes into me. I'm hot, so hot. The sweat is pouring off me. My head is pounding with the poppers.

I moan around the obstruction of the mask – beg you to take me, own me, transform me…

You stand up and turn me over. My eyes are filled with the expanse of the rubber sheets. They squeak under my hot writhing body.

Looking over my shoulder, I can see you lubing up the sheath on your cock – it shines with the moisture, and seems to throb in time with my hot arse, with the shared panting rhythm of our connected breath. My arse burns as I feel you push your fingers in, guiding that shining member to my waiting hole. Slowly you push it in, thrusting slowly, heavily into me.

I take another heady draw on the connecting tube of poppers and my skin responds with fire. I'm moaning and twisting, as you push in and out: taking me, taking my arse, filling me. I can feel your legs against mine, rubber squealing – your hands on my arse, feeling around to my aching cock and balls.

You pull me up from the bed. Your hands pull and twist my cock and balls whilst your cock buries itself deeper in me – filling me, pushing me closer.

In the mirror before us, I can see our shining bodies merging, becoming one. Already it is hard to tell us apart: two rubber clad bodies, two hooded heads, glass eye pieces staring – the connecting tube an umbilical cord between us.

I feel myself joined to you: my arse is filled with your hard cock, my balls surrounded by your gloved fist; even my ears are filled with the sound of your breathing, and my lungs filled half with poppers, and half with your own exhalations. As you push harder into me, I feel myself slipping away, I feel the excitement, the rush of poppers combining in my blood: merging with the latex skin that surrounds and contains me, defines me.

My skin, my arse, my cock, my eyes and throat, begin to burn with transformation.

I feel the latex begin to tighten and shrink around me, begin to penetrate me. As the rubber skin slides down my throat, and coats my mouth, my teeth, my eyes, I feel it also begin to take control of me.

I can feel myself becoming, transforming. I am being sealed in, absorbed by my new rubber skin and my own desire.

But I am not alone…

I feel your hard cock kick and pulse within me; my own cock throbs in time to its persistence. I feel that familiar rise of excitement. Through the fog of my disoriented, transforming mind I know I'm going to come, to fill my suit.

I hear you mutter encouragement, swearing through gritted teeth:

"*Come on boy, fill that suit for me: pump my cock with your arse!*"

I feel you swell inside me; I know you are on the edge too.

You drive and push harder. My arse is on fire, and my cock burns. The poppers make my head reel, my mouth is dry and my legs are giving way, but I push myself back onto you harder, force you into me deeper.

I'm becoming one with you: one flesh joined at the crotch and mouth. I know that now I'm truly becoming a RUBBERMAN, and with the last of my will I embrace the change.

With a final shudder and gasp, the earth spins as I come like I've never done before…

"…there is a dog inside of me. A pure, simple animal – devoid of guilt or shame…"

Dog

Preparation

There is a dog inside of me.

An animal that quietly hides beneath the layers of humanity and convention.

A pure, simple animal – devoid of guilt or shame.

An animal that knows instinctively what I want and need.

––––––––––

The dog inside of me knows that I need to be released in order to truly find myself.

That I need to be broken of my social conditioning, my 'normality', and humanity so that I can surrender to the real me: the primal animal inside of me.

The dog inside knows that I secretly yearn to feel a rubber skin surround me. To feel a hood enclose my head and hide my face, and tight smooth mitts transform my hands to paws.

It knows that I am happiest when on all fours and at my Masters feet – knows that I would truly be happiest when I have finally become his lovingly devoted hound: well trained, obedient and happy.

The dog in me knows that my soft human body needs special training in order to learn to conform to Master's demands. That it needs to learn to yearn for the touch of His hands through the rubber skin, the pull of Master's hands around its cock and balls, to feel the comforting tightness of His collar and chain around its neck…

It knows that my mouth is only going to be happy when it can taste the oiled leather of Master's boots – and the smooth curve of His jeans as they cup His crotch and arse… It knows that I will only feel pleasure when He finally gives me permission to lick at the salty tang of His cock.

The dog in me knows that I want to be trained to please my Master: to worship Him, body and soul. Because through Him the dog in me is made real, made whole…

It is the dog inside of me that knows that this body needs to be reprogrammed to feel all of this as pleasure – to come to need it like the food it laps up from its bowl, or the air that it breaths through the holes in the mask.

That it needs to be trained from merely liking rubber and leather, to needing it to survive. To needing its Master like it needs air – and to worship and love Him and everything He does to it for this.

———

All of this is more than I am now.

Now I love to wear my rubber, to play a little rough – a little bondage and breath-play sometimes, a little SM…

But *this* is different.

This part of me needs more – *wants* more; and wants to be made into an animal that NEEDS more too.

This part of me knows that it needs to shed its conditioning to the point where it becomes simply an animal – a rubber dog. The loving, devoted pet of my Master, to use as He sees fit…

Induction

Sir.

Master.

I found myself thinking of you today – and of all that I could become with your help.

I called up the pictures you had emailed me, and then found myself kneeling on the floor – looking up into your bearded face, seeing your intense eyes staring into the camera – and through it into me…

It made me shudder with excitement and longing.

Because, Sir, I long to be kneeling at your feet: to be able to stare up at you with hunger and devotion as I lick your hand and nuzzle my face into your open palm.

It would thrill me to have you smile down at me and tousle my hair – affectionately pleased with your obedient and loving dog…

Sir – I long to come into your presence – to have your calm voice tell me to kneel before you, and to tremble as you lock your collar around my neck. To feel your possession and ownership in that act, but also the freedom that your collar means to me.

I need to have those powerful, steady eyes stare deep into mine – to feel myself falling deeper and deeper into their bottomless, calm stare.

To feel myself quietly slipping away as I hear your calm voice telling me that I can let go of my fear, let go of my uncertainties. That you will now take care of me…

Telling me that I must no longer worry: because you are now in control, and you will make sure that nothing can ever harm me.

I need to feel the power of your presence. To hear your voice, and see your calm stare – to feel my breathing deepen as you slowly help me to relax – entrancing me as I sink down, become calm, become receptive…

I know that what you say is true: that with you I can relax – that I can allow all of my fears to subside and give way – that your calm voice and deep eyes will hold everything safe for me as I gently let everything drift.

That I can safely surrender everything to you in trust and confidence…

I feel myself falling into your eyes – feel my chin rest in the palm of your hand as you hold my head steady. Find myself unable to lock away from your eyes, or stop straining to hear your quiet, calm voice…

Your voice that is telling me how in the past I have been foolish – and I know that it is true.

That I have been frightened by how powerful and overwhelming my desires can sometimes be. That I have felt unable to control them, and so they govern me still.

But you tell me that you can help me: that you can control these desires – if I let you, if I give you the power. That you can master them for me: if I surrender my control to you.

Your voice is quiet and calm, your hands are steady: one cupping my chin, the other stroking my cheek. Your voice is gentle as it quietly tells me that you can be the force that will govern these desires, and in governing them set me free from them.

And as I gaze into your steady eyes – feeling so beautifully calm and relaxed – I realise that it is true, that you know the truth. I know that you can help me – that I want you to help me, that I *need* you to help me…

I feel my head grow heavy in your supporting hand, feel myself physically starting to lean onto you – surrendering to your calm voice, your deep eyes, and the whispered promise of safety that they hold…

As I physically surrender, I feel myself emotionally relax too – and hear you encourage me, praise me – tell me that I am doing the right thing, that I can no longer help myself, that you will control the desires – and through them, me…

And in the beautifully warm, relaxed and calm state that washes through me, I know that you are right: that you can control these urges and passions, that you can master them.

And I know that this means that you can be a Master to *me* too – and so I feel something inside of me melt and give – a boundary that seems to dissolve, somewhere deep inside of me… I give a little shudder and a sigh as I feel a flood of energy and power that flows from the core of me and into you. And as I let myself flow into you, into the warmth of your hands, I know only that I want you to help me, want you to control these passions.

I feel myself fading away: all my fears, all my strength, all my old life – slipping away into your eyes and your voice. Feel my mind and body relax ever deeper – sink down until I am held up by your hand where it cups my chin…

And as I sink in peace and pleasure, I can see a beautiful smile that creep into your eyes, across your face: and I am happy that I have made you smile…

Then your voice is telling me to relax further, to surrender to the warmth and pleasure, and let myself go completely.

Telling me that I am feeling sleepy now, that I am falling into a deep sleep… and I realise that I am so *tired*…

I feel my eyes droop under the suggestion of your voice – feel myself drifting into a warm, relaxed sleepy state – and I let myself drift because I know that I can trust you, that I can give myself over to you – because then you can help me…

And I do so want you to help me, I so want to please you…

These are the last thoughts that go through my head as I drift down into blissful sleep…

Entranced

I find myself floating in a warm sense of well being.

I feel disembodied, weightless (*even though a part of me knows that I still kneel at your feet, with my chin resting in your palm, and your collar padlocked around my neck…*)

My mind is completely focused on your calm, firm voice as it speaks to me of all my secret desires – and at the sound, I feel my mind drift into what I think is a wonderful and erotic dream…

…I dream that you tell me that you now have complete control of my desires, and through them, of my body.

I feel weak, heavy – and in that weakness realise that you are right: that I can no longer move from my relaxed state…

As this is a dream, I do not worry or fight the sensation – I have had strange dreams before, and this must just be another wild dream fantasy. In a distant part of my mind, the thought comes that I will wake soon, so I might as well enjoy it whilst it lasts…

I dream that you are telling me that you have total power over me – that I have surrendered everything to you: my fears, my desires, my mind… and in the dream I know that this is true, that I want to surrender – and so I relax and let you take control…

And then I dream that you are telling me that as you now control my desires, I can finally let them go. And so I find myself quietly confessing every wild thought and fantasy I have ever had: the secret desires for being encased and bound in rubber; the heady, shameful excitement of feeling my body restricted, enfolded and helpless; my fearful hunger to be encased in hoods and gas masks and the total surrender of breath control and poppers; the way I love to sprawl on the floor at a man's feet so that I can rub my face and tongue into his boot leather or the slick peppery rubber of his waders: happily drooling as I work my tongue into the lacing, the soles and the cleats. I find my voice shakes as I confess of my desire to worship a man's crotch: to feel him fill my mouth and my senses with the masculine swell of his power – and an even deeper shame in wanting to bury my long tongue into his arse…

And then I finally confess my secret desire to learn the joys of water sports: to know the warm scent of his piss as it fills my mouth, drips off my face and beard, and runs down my chest.

Confess the shameful need to have my body trained to become hungry for another man – the need to be dependent on him for sexual release – the hunger to feel him own me, control me – to know that my body, mouth and hole are his…

As I confess, I feel something inside of me give way.

As I tell of my shame, confess my desires to you, I feel those negative emotions slip away – feel myself become free in the telling – that in the acceptance of my desires I am truly released from them.

That feeling of release feels good – feels horny… *so horny…*

Through my whole confession, your voice quietly encourages me – reminds me that the hornier I feel, the weaker I feel – and the more I feel the need to surrender…

As your voice croons at me I feel your hands touch and stroke me… and it feels so good, so horny that I relax even more… and I give myself over to the feelings… surrender even more…

…and the more I surrender, the more free I feel – and the freer I feel, the less I need to think…

I sink and surrender, and find myself becoming only sensation and pleasure… until soon there is *only* the pleasure and your voice – calm, steady, hypnotic… and the slow rhythmic stroke of your hand on my chin…

————

Now, in the dream, you are telling me a new thing – a good thing…

You tell me that I have surrendered so much to you that I am blissfully free of all my doubts and my fears – that I am free of all my restrictions.

That I have surrendered so much of myself that I am really no longer even truly human…

And your voice tells me that this is a *good* thing: because now I can finally let go of everything, and truly embrace the animal inside of me that is just waiting to be let out.

And since I know that this is a dream, I find that I readily believe you.

And so it also makes sense when you tell me that because I have surrendered so much, I am now really little more than a small animal – like a loving puppy before his Master… and I find that in the dream what you say makes so much sense…

And to confirm how much sense this makes, your voice tells me that I must be a puppy – or else why would I be wearing a puppy's collar…?

And at your words, my mind becomes aware of the tight leather strap that is buckled around my neck, and that you are right: that I am like a little pet to you – and with a simple minded excitement I realise how good that feels – and that being a pet just feels right…

And then your voice tells me that I am a good puppy, a good dog – and that you will take care of me and be my Master… And I like that:

I like the sound of my Master's voice, and the touch of his hand upon my head, stroking my hair and my chin… and I want to tell my Master how good it feels – but I find I can only make a small barking noise…

But then realise that's OK: since dogs don't actually talk after all…

And now my Master is telling me that a well-behaved puppy should be on the floor – and I know that Master is right, so in the dream I go down on all fours, and give a doggy smile when my Master pats me and says "*Good boy!*"

I feel good here on the floor at Master's feet – but my front feet feel wrong: they're too long somehow… and my skin feels naked and exposed… and so my doggy brain feels uncomfortable and I give a little whine…

But then my Master tells me to roll over and stick my paws in the air so that he can put my puppy coat on…

I roll over and watch with excitement whilst Master carefully pulls a tight, shiny coat over my back paws and then works it up along and over my body. The coat is smooth, tight, and glossy black – it feels a little cold and smells very strongly of rubber.

Master tells me that I like the tightness and the heady smell – that it makes me feel good to be wearing my rubber coat. He tells me that without it I would feel cold and lonely. I find that Master is right: that in the tight closeness of the new coat I feel better than I ever have felt before… I love my Master for showing me this, and I wriggle a little to help him as he pulls the suit up and over me, over my back. At his command, I then obediently slip my front legs into the suit, and then sit still whilst he finally pulls it closed with a nice big zip across my shoulders…

…and I find that the suit has helped my front feet too – because as they slip down inside the sleeves they slide into nicely tight padded rubber mitts. The mitts even have little rubber paw-shaped pads on the underside – they turn my ugly long front feet back into proper paws, just like a puppy should have – and I feel really happy that this is so…

Master smiles as he looks me over – then ruffles my hair and tells me that as I am a real puppy now, I should have a proper puppy muzzle… and so I lean forward, resting my shoulder against His leg whilst he pulls more of the shiny coat up and over my head. Like the rest of my lovely coat, it is tight and smooth and it feels good as it snaps into place around my naked face. I find that I can't hear so well, and I can only see a little – but Master tells me that I look like a proper doggy now, and so I am happy that I have pleased him…

Master then strokes and touches my new coat all over – pulling and stretching it so that it fits in all the right places. As it snugs into place I feel very good: I can feel the warmth of Master's hands through the coat, and it makes me shudder with excitement… Master tells me that this is because my new coat is a better skin than the old one: that its tightness makes it easier for me to feel and respond to his touch, and its glossy shine shows off my body and its reactions so that he can instantly see how much his pup likes what he does.

He tells me that this new coat helps to hold my body in the right way: that it keeps my back straight and my head held high – a proud glossy pup showing its man how happy it is to be his.

He tells me that I really want this glossy coat to be my real skin – and I find that he is right: without this skin I felt naked and lonely – but within its tight embrace I know that my Master loves me, and so I am happy…

Then Master tells me to come and sit at his feet – so I do – and I nuzzle my new face into his hand, and lick his palm for him, as a good dog should…

I want to do anything for him to show him how much I love him.

My Master tells me that he will train me – since all good dogs must be trained.

And I trust him, and know that what my Master wants is right – that it will make me feel good to be trained – and that it will make me a real pet dog: one he can proudly show off to other Masters…

————

Somewhere, in the dim reaches of my mind, a part of me watches this dream take place, and enjoys the wild fantasies I can call up – a part of me that waits for the dream to end and for me to wake up…

…and waits…

…and waits – whilst this new rubber-puppy slowly becomes one with the dog-mind that has been created from his old personality… the dog-mind that gently swamps and then rewires his old human brain…

The dog-mind that is slowly trained to serve his new Master:

…trained to become one with his rubber-skin: permanently sealed into the suit and the paws and the hood – and trained to be so excited about the way his new rubber skin makes him feel;

…trained to adapt to his new position on all fours; trained until his body adjusts and adapts – evolves into a new permanent and irreversible state;

….trained to be obedient: to sit, to lie, to fetch and to walk to heel when his Master takes him for walks to the clubs and bars – trained to sit patiently at his feet whilst he talks to all his other Master friends – and proudly shows off his new puppy to them;

…trained to love and worship and lick his Master's boots and body;

…trained to roll over and let Master stroke and play with every part of his puppy's body whenever Master wants…

Trained to love and worship his new Master like the air that he breathes and the food that he eats from his own special bowl.

Trained to love his Master like no man ever could.

To love him like only a true dog can: as Man's best friend…

Trained to forget that there was ever anything other than this service and this love of his Master – or that there was ever any other skin than the tight rubber that confines and defines his world.

Trained to be his Master's pet, his dog – always and forever…

Because – outside of the dream-that-is-not-a-dream that is what the puppy that was once me has now become: Sir's dog, Sir's pet – Sir's loving rubber canine companion.

Unaware and uncaring of any life that I might have had before Sir took away the shame and the care – and made him what I now am:

My Master's faithful and devoted rubber dog: and happier than I have ever been.

"…I want you to need the rubber – hunger for it to be your skin…"

Mesmerized

God these rubber shorts feel good.

Even when sitting still I can feel the tight restriction of them against my thighs – and the slight 'give' at my crotch. I barely dare move – 'cos every time I do I feel the wet slipperiness of my own sweat and pre-cum bathing my dick where it is securely held in its dark rubbery prison…

The weird thing is that I don't actually remember leaving them on this morning!

I remember thinking about putting on some rubber whilst doing my morning work-out – getting a buzz from the thought of how my muscles would feel: so warm and sweaty within the tight rubber – but the first thing I knew that I still had them on was when I felt the building warmth and pressure as I walked to work. It's odd, but I guess I must have just zoned out when getting dressed, and forgotten to take 'em off again. It was a weird feeling checking myself in the mirror in the Gents here at work: pulling down my jeans to find the shiny black rubber coating my legs and sticking out from under my boxer shorts

– çeez: I guess must have actually put those on over the top of the rubber. I am such a lame brain!!

I shift again in my seat – and thank the rubber-gods that I have my own office when I hear that all too familiar 'squelch' of warm, wet rubber.

I guess it's the shorts – but I'm also finding it really hard to concentrate on my work: I've got Messenger open in one window and one of the fetish profile sites in another – it's almost like I'm waiting for something…

Like I say – I guess it's just the shorts turning me on and making me distracted…

Wait a mo – my luck is in: who's this messaging me…?

> [session start]
>
> *Mesmerize:* hello there…
>
> *Rubber_O:* how-do
>
> *Mesmerize:* fine, fine - yourself?
>
> *Rubber_O:* err, great thanks…
>
> *Rubber_O:* um - sorry, but - do I know you?
>
> *Mesmerize:* I'm not sure - why?
>
> *Rubber_O:* it's just weird - I kinda feel like I might know you but I don't remember your nic… hehe - sorry, it's probably me: I've been a bit "out of it" today {grin}
>
> *Mesmerize:* really? Do you want to talk about it?

Rubber_O: nah – you'll think I'm daft…!

Mesmerize: that's ok – I just thought you might want to share ;)

Rubber_O: I'm just a bit distracted I guess – I seem to be forgetting things this morning – doing weird stuff.

Mesmerize: sounds fun! – Like what?

Rubber_O: like putting on the wrong underwear!! Hehehe

Mesmerize: now you have got my interest boy! – explain!

Rubber_O: ooh – yes Sir! Except it kinda means making a confession… {embarrassed look}

Mesmerize: hehe – you can confide in me Rubber_O if you like – if you feel you can trust me.

Rubber_O: kinda feels weird, but I do feel like I *can* trust you…

Rubber_O: OK – I've got a bit of a thing for rubber, and this morning I find that I've come into work with my rubber shorts still on under my work clothes! {blush}

Mesmerize: sounds interesting boy! Don't you do that often then?

Rubber_O: not that often Sir – I find that it distracts me.

Mesmerize: they make you feel good do they boy?

Rubber_O: exactly Sir!

Mesmerize: all that nice tight, slippery rubber holding you snug and warm, eh?

Rubber_O: hmmm - god yes Sir!

Mesmerize: hehe - that's good, boy - isn't it?

Rubber_O: god Sir, yes Sir! *Thank you Sir*!

Mesmerize: nice response, boy!

Rubber_O: geez - sorry. I'm not sure I know where that came from!!

Mesmerize: It just kinda bubbled up from deep inside you did it? From down in that damp warm rubbery space inside…?

Rubber_O: umph - yes Sir!

Rubber_O: like I say, I guess I'm just not myself this morning!

Mesmerize: the question is, boy - do you like how you're feeling? Do you want to stay feeling this way?

Rubber_O: Yes Sir - I do like this feeling Sir!

Mesmerize: I thought so boy: you like the warm spreading feeling in your crotch - the soft feeling of the rubber holding you tight and secure…

Rubber_O: oh god yes Sir! Warm, soft and so horny!

Mesmerize: maybe that is why you left the shorts on this morning, boy? Because you felt the need to stay in that warm relaxed state - because you wanted to feel that warmth spreading through your body all day…

Rubber_O: yes Sir - I remember now: that is exactly how it felt this morning - the rubber felt so warm, so much a part of me that I didn't want it to end!

Mesmerize: tell me how you feel now boy.

Rubber_O: Sir - I feel really good Sir - I feel warm and secure Sir - it's like the rubber is enfolding me and relaxing me, Sir!

Rubber_O: Sir - I also feel good talking to you.

Mesmerize: that's good boy - I'm glad that you feel good talking to me like this - it feels good to open up and talk sometimes, doesn't it boy?

Rubber_O: yes Sir, it does - very good! I do feel very good, now Sir - very relaxed. Gods, but it's been a while since I felt this good - this relaxed and comfortable…

Mesmerize: I'm pleased that you feel that way boy - pleased that I can be here for you like this.

Rubber_O: thank you Sir - thank you for talking to me and making me feel so good like this.

Rubber_O: I wish more of my friends were like you Sir.

Mesmerize: Do you not feel close to your friends boy?

Rubber_O: I thought I did Sir, but lately they seem to have been really getting on my back – always wanting me to go out and do stuff with them.

Rubber_O: they don't appreciate that I've actually got my own stuff to do…

Mesmerize: that's a shame boy – are they also into rubber?

Rubber_O: no Sir – they don't really know about my rubber "thing" Sir.

Mesmerize: so it's just our little secret…?

Rubber_O: yes Sir - I don't tell anyone else - I'm too embarrassed and shy {blush}

Mesmerize: you know there is no need to feel like that with me boy.

Rubber_O: No Sir! I feel I can trust you Sir – you seem to understand me so well!

Mesmerize: is that how it feels boy?

Rubber_O: yes Sir - like you understand me - like you can see into me and understand all about me. It's a good feeling Sir.

Mesmerize: I'm pleased you feel like that boy – that it feels good for you to open up to me like this.

Rubber_0: yes Sir – feels good to open up to you – it seems so easy to talk to you Sir – as if I've known you all my life…

Mesmerize: as if I was a part of you – and you a part of me…

Rubber_0: yes Sir – as if I was a part of you… I want to please you Sir.

Mesmerize: good boy!

Rubber_0: yes Sir – thank you Sir!

Mesmerize: how does that make you feel boy?

Rubber_0: very good Sir – like waves of arousal and relaxation through me Sir – like the rubber ripples over my skin when I read those words…

Mesmerize: GOOD – you are coming along nicely…

Rubber_0: Sorry, Sir..?

Mesmerize: nothing boy…

Mesmerize: it's a shame your friends don't understand you, but I guess that happens sometimes – people change, and their friends don't always understand that… I guess we all reach a time when we eventually outgrow our friends…

Rubber_0: true Sir – but you are always here for me, Sir – and You make me feel so much better than they ever did.

Mesmerize: thank you boy! That means a lot to me.

Rubber_O: I mean it Sir – you are a true friend – I feel I could spend my whole time with you…

Rubber_O: Sir, I feel I want to spend my time with you…

Rubber_O: time with you, Sir – and time in rubber: feeling this good, feeling this open – feeling this rubbery and pliant…

Mesmerize: that is very good boy – it makes me feel very proud!

Rubber_O: oh, thank you Sir – that makes me feel so good!

Mesmerize: good…!

Mesmerize: **BOY: YOUR LEASH IS READY**

Rubber_O: Sir: I am your property and pet. I am yours to control.

Mesmerize: good boy

Mesmerize: boy – tell me how you feel.

Rubber_O: Sir, I am here as you commanded, Sir.

Rubber_O: Sir, I am ready for your commands – I am eager to serve you, Sir.

Mesmerize: good boy – it seems that the triggers we planted have worked perfectly.

Mesmerize: now boy — I want you to listen to my Voice and to obey: you feel so good obeying me, don't you boy?

Rubber_O: Sir, I feel so good obeying you Sir.

Mesmerize: GOOD BOY

Mesmerize: now listen boy — I have used the trigger I planted in you and you are now so relaxed — so eager to please — feeling so very warm and secure… you do feel so good now, don't you boy?

Rubber_O: Sir, yes Sir — so warm and relaxed sir.

Mesmerize: good. And every time we talk like this — every time you listen to my Voice and I take you under: you go deeper and deeper — you feel more and more relaxed — more and more open to me — don't you boy?

Rubber_O: yes Sir — more and more open to you Sir.

Mesmerize: GOOD BOY

Mesmerize: you will continue wanting to meet me on-line boy — you like the feeling of being entranced, of being controlled so much. But you won't carry any conscious memory of our chats, will you boy?

Rubber_O: No Sir — need to talk to you Sir, but won't remember you Sir…

Mesmerize: that's good boy – forgetting helps me to deepen your programming. Your obedience and eagerness to obey pleases me very much, boy. You like to obey and to please me, don't you boy?

Rubber_O: Sir, yes Sir!! I live to obey and to please you Sir!

Mesmerize: that is good boy – that is because obedience is what you were made for, boy. That is all that you want from your life now, isn't it boy? – You live to serve and obey me now, don't you boy…?

Rubber_O: yes Sir! I live to obey and to please you Sir!

Mesmerize: no-one else understands you like I do boy – no-one else understands this need in you – this need to be owned and to serve – to be obedient and mindless.

Rubber_O: Sir, I am yours to command Sir – I live only for you Sir!

Mesmerize: and why is that boy? Tell your Master what you are boy?

Rubber_O: Sir – I am your slave Sir!

Mesmerize: yes boy – you are my slave, boy – my hypnotically re-programmed slave.

Rubber_O: Sir, thank you for making me your slave Sir.

Mesmerize: GOOD BOY!

Mesmerize: does the slave like what its Master has done to him?

Rubber_O: Master, Sir – slave is made complete by your programming Sir!

Mesmerize: Good boy – good slave.

Rubber_O: Master – slave knows its true place now – that it is a slave; that it lives to serve and to please you – that it lives to become what you command of it Sir!

Mesmerize: yes slave – you want only to become whatever I desire of you, don't you slave?

Rubber_O: yes Sir! I am your slave Sir. Please Sir, command your slave Sir!

Mesmerize: you are hungry to serve, aren't you slave?

Rubber_O: yes Sir! I am your slave Sir – please Sir, command your slave Sir!

Mesmerize: GOOD BOY!

Mesmerize: listen to my Will, Slave:

Mesmerize: you will continue to wait on-line for me every day at this time boy – as you have done every day for the last 3 months. But you will have no conscious recollection of ever having talked to me – you will not even recognise my nic on the screen.

Mesmerize: you will continue to wear rubber whenever you can boy: you will feel the need for it building up in you; you need to feel the warm, relaxed restriction of rubber on your body – the rubber that makes you feel pliant and open and empty… You find that wearing rubber makes you feel so relaxed, yet so horny too… You need the rubber, and you need to talk to me whilst wearing rubber…

Mesmerize: Do you understand boy?

Rubber_O: yes Sir – I will wear my rubber every day – even at work under my clothes Sir.

Rubber_O: wearing my rubber makes me feel good Sir – it makes me feel more of a slave Sir.

Mesmerize: yes slave – GOOD BOY! – That is what the rubber is for boy – what I have programmed the rubber to do to you boy: to make you need and want to be a slave whenever you wear it for me.

Mesmerize: I want you to need the rubber – hunger for it to be your skin. Because the rubber makes you feel good – the rubber makes you feel complete. Wearing rubber makes you want to BE rubber.

Rubber_O: yes Sir – I want to be rubber for you, Sir.

Mesmerize: GOOD BOY. You will continue to meet me boy – to obey and need to obey. You need to feel this open, this deep – this under my control, don't you boy?

Rubber_O: yes Sir – to obey and to be controlled Sir!

Rubber_O: Sir – when can I come to you Sir? When will I be ready for you to take me Sir?

Mesmerize: patience, boy – not yet. First you must need me more than anything else in your life, boy – need to serve me more than life itself… I want you to need me, and need the rubber. Can you do that for me boy?

Rubber_O: Sir, yes Sir! I need you Sir – I need to serve you Sir!!

Rubber_O: Sir – I need to be your slave for real Sir: I need to feel that complete surrender as you take everything from me, Sir – as you wipe my mind clean and help me become what I am Sir: your perfect slave in rubber Sir!

Mesmerize: boy, you do not know how happy it makes me to read those words!

Rubber_O: thank you Sir! It makes me feel so good to know that you are happy with me Sir.

Mesmerize: boy – I am more than happy – I am *proud*.

Rubber_O: thank you Sir!! I live only to serve and make you proud Sir! Please Sir: command your boy – take your slave Sir!

Mesmerize: I will be proud to take you slave – to have you here with me forever – serving me, loving me, obeying me without question…

Mesmerize: I will take you soon boy – have you here so that I can complete your training and then implant your new slave personality so completely that it overwrites everything of who you once where…

Mesmerize: you want to be my total slave, don't you boy? To serve me completely and to surrender your whole life and mind to me…?

Rubber_O: please, Sir! My life and my mind are yours Sir – please Sir, take them and remake me as you wish!

Mesmerize: a little while yet boy – I am rewriting your mind, and that takes time! These things must be taken slowly. Savour this time of learning and growing, boy: just as I savour each piece of you that I shave from your mind…

Mesmerize: but to complete my work I need you alone for greater periods of time – alone and rubbered. Alone and waiting for me. Open to me, to the rubber and to my commands…

Rubber_O: yes Sir – rubbered, open and yours alone, Sir!

Mesmerize: GOOD BOY! I need to separate you further from your friends now, boy – or they will interfere with your programming. They don't understand you like I do boy; they will want to try and stop you – to come between you and me boy – between you and how good you feel with me…

Rubber_O: Sir, I need you Sir – I need to feel this good with you Sir!

Mesmerize: GOOD BOY – of course you need to feel this good with me boy. You are my slave, boy, and a slave is only truly alive when he is with his Master, and being His slave.

Rubber_O: yes Master. I am a slave, Master. I am YOUR slave, Master.

Mesmerize: good boy – GOOD SLAVE!

Mesmerize: now boy – it's time for you to go back: but don't worry – even though you will not consciously remember this conversation, you will still carry the memory of my triggers deep inside you – deep in your subconscious where they will continue to change you – continue rewriting your mind from within. And the need to obey my triggers and commands will still be ingrained deep into your core…

Rubber_O: Master I am yours.

Mesmerize: GOOD BOY

Mesmerize: now boy: **INTO THE BOX**

Rubber_O: into the box, Sir…

Mesmerize: hey mate – you ok?

Rubber_O: sorry…? Ah, yeah – I'm fine…. I guess I must've just zoned out for a while again there!

Rubber_O: Sorry {grin} Where we saying anything important…?

Mesmerize: sounds like you need a coffee! I better let you go – I'm sure you must have a million things needing doing.

Rubber_O: sure – if I can get my mind fixed onto anything besides these dammed shorts! {guilty grin}

Mesmerize: I'm sure you will: hopefully I'll see you around sometime…?

Rubber_O: I guess… sorry I've been a bit 'off' mate – but I hope you had fun anyway…

Mesmerize: trust me buddy – I had more fun than you can ever realise…

[session end]

Huh! – what a weird thing to say before signing off… you meet some of the weirdest people on-line sometimes!

Still, he seemed a nice guy – it might be fun to chat to him again…

Shit – if only I could remember what his nic was…?

"…I am a rubber droid – the property and pet of my Master…"

Droid

I am a rubber-droid.

I know this because the *Voice* tells me so.

The *Voice* is my teacher, my guru and Master. What it tells me I know to be true. What it orders, I must obey. Obeying the *Voice* is pure pleasure to me. Obeying the *Voice* makes my body quiver and tremble.

It feels good to obey the *Voice*. It is my duty, my destiny and my pleasure.

The *Voice* is always here with me – but it is most insistent when my Master stores me away at night. The *Voice's* quiet, calm words repeat themselves endlessly then, as I lie in the darkness of His workroom – they swirl and echo around the open and empty chambers of my rubbered mind, weaving a web of obedience and surrender that lulls me down into sleep...

The *Voice* is my programming. It tells me who I am, what I exist for, how I am to function:

"You are a rubber-droid.
You are receptive to programming.
You are the property and pet of your Master.
You exist to please and serve your Master.

Your leash is ready:
Relax and submit to your Master, droid.

You are a rubber-droid.
You are the property and pet of your Master.
Your leash is ready:
Relax and submit to your Master, droid…"

This is what the *voice* tells me. It repeats these words over and over. My robotic dreams are filled with them. They repeat themselves quietly in my head even when awake.

These words have become my entire world. They are the only truth I know:

I am a rubber-droid.

I am the property and pet of my Master.

I exist to please and serve my Master.

My robotic mind is empty and receptive to His commands.

Every touch or word from Him fills my robotic being with pleasure.

I owe everything to my Master. Everything I need, want or desire comes from Him.

My Master created my rubber-body and programmed my robotic mind.

I am His creation and His masterpiece. Everything that I am is made by Him: sculpted in perfection and designed for His service. My entire body – bones, skin, even teeth – is made of shiny, black, pliant rubber. I am naked and hairless, so that my Master may appreciate the beauty of the body that He has created to serve Him.

I surrender everything to my master – to my Creator.

Although my resting state is humanoid in shape, my rubber body is pliant and adaptable – it can be reformed on command to any shape or specification: mannequin, furniture, man or dog. I feel intense pleasure when my Master alters my body to conform to His will in this way.

This rubber body is also capable of intense sensory feedback: the slightest touch from my Master's hand gives me orgasmic pleasure; every word He speaks fills me with love and well-being. My Master designed and programmed me this way. I love my Master for giving me such pleasure in obeying His commands.

I exist to please and serve my Master. It is my only purpose and my only pleasure.

————

I remember the first time I was allowed to see my new rubber body – freshly created and standing before the mirrors that line the Master's workshop. I remember the dazzle as the lights reflected from my shiny black skin. I remember being strangely excited at the sight of that completely smooth, seamless rubber body.

I remember marvelling at its perfection: the sculpted chest, the muscular shoulders and swelling biceps, the perfect 'V' of its back and its narrow hips, the ridged perfection of its abs.

The rubber shone and gleamed, and as my body moved under my Master's commands I could see the way it stretched and reformed itself perfectly around every mound and shape. The glossy coating only emphasised every detail: drawing the eye to every muscle, tendon and vein.

I remember my strange excitement at seeing this rubber-skinned form. I remember a feeling of metamorphosis – almost as if there had been a time when this body had looked different, felt different…

Even now, years later, there are times when that feeling comes over me again – I catch the reflected image of my glossy body as it obediently performs a task, and I feel myself shudder with a strange dislocation of identity that leaves me feeling that I might not always have been this creature of obedient rubber perfection.

It disturbs me when I feel like this.

I tell my Master when these emotions rise. He tells me that these feelings are small glitches in my programming, and then He takes me down into his workshop to reprogram me and return me to my blissful state of rubber identity and obedience…

After reprogramming, I am remade as my Master's creation again – fully assimilated to His command.

––––––––

There is a large rubber-topped bench in the centre of my Master's workshop. Banks of computers and instruments surround it. There are also many mirrors. When my Master places me on the bench, I can see myself reflected from many angles; Master says this is essential for the sensory feedback that re-affirms His programming.

My Master spends some time connecting me to the various instruments and computers – He attaches wires to my fingers and pads to my chest. Sometimes He places instruments and tubes right inside my body – most often this includes an object within my anal cavity. Sometimes it also means tubes inserted into every other orifice. I am not sure if I enjoy that part – but my Master tells me it is necessary, and so I obey Him and lie very still whilst He works…

The final piece of equipment is always a large metallic helmet that encases my head. Within the helmet is a small screen. My Master flashes images upon this screen. Sometimes these are live video feeds from various cameras in the workshop; sometimes they are recordings from previous sessions…

The *Voice* echoes within the helmet as the images flash across the screen. It states my full programming: affirmations of my name, state and purpose, lists of orders and commands and my programmed response to them…

The *Voice* repeats this programming over and over.

The flashing images work in harmony with the *Voice*. Sometimes they illustrate what the *Voice* is saying. They show rubber-skinned creatures like myself. Sometimes I think they might be me, sometimes they show real men in rubber. The men seem to be very excited about their rubber clothing. Sometimes the rubber they wear is so tight that it is as if they have a rubber skin like me.

Some of these men act as if they are androids. These are the images that I like the best. It is strangely exciting for me to see real men pretending to be rubber-droids; to see them covering their pink skins in tight black suits, hiding their heads behind hoods and gas masks of rubber. Obeying commands…

————

I do not know why, but there is one set of images that excites me most. It shows a young bearded man with short dark hair. He lies upon a bench very like my Master's workbench. He is limp, and his eyes are open but blank. He appears to be drugged. There is a look of intense but relaxed pleasure on his face.

A man comes. He is tall, in full tight rubber and a long rubber apron. He wears heavy boots, long gloves and a hood.

For a moment, he stands beside the bench. He reaches out a gloved hand and strokes the youth's cheek, trails his finger across his jaw and down his chest. The young man moans quietly, tips his head and arches his back in pleasure.

The Rubberman gently takes the young man's wrists and fastens them to the bench. He does the same with his feet. The young man is stretched out: spread-eagled. Vulnerable. Helpless…

The Rubberman takes out an electric shaver – it buzzes as the blades slide over the young man's body; where it passes you can see the hair fall away. The Rubberman works slowly and purposefully. He passes the shaver over every inch of the restrained body: his feet, his legs, his chest and arms – even his groin and arse.

The Rubberman leaves the young man's head until last. The hair falls thick and dark as the blades buzz over his skull…

The Rubberman carefully starts to apply a white astringent cream to the young man's naked body. As the cream eats into the skin, it dissolves the remaining hair and permanently burns out the follicles. For a moment the youth's calm face twitches in pain. The Rubberman notices this; he places a breathing apparatus over the grimacing face and there is the hiss of gas. When he takes the mask away from the young man's face, his eyes are closed and he seems more relaxed.

The Rubberman returns to applying the hair-removal cream – coating even the man's head and face. When he removes the cream, the restrained body is completely hairless.

The camera focuses in on the young man's body. His restrained body shines smooth and naked under the lights. He looks somehow less human...

————————

The images flash: now they show the young man standing with his arms out to the sides.

As the camera watches, a patch of grey appears on his naked stomach. It spreads and grows, slowly covering his entire torso. The Rubberman comes into view: he holds an airbrush, and carefully applies layer upon layer of liquid latex to the young man's still and silent form. As each layer dries, it goes from pale grey to deep glossy black.

Each layer makes the young man's features less distinct.

Each layer removes more of his identity.

Each layer makes his naked and hairless body appear more like that of an android...

I feel a stir of excitement as I lie upon my Master's workbench and watch these images. There is something strangely familiar about them – in seeing the slow transformation of this young man's pink human form to something resembling the seamless and glossy black perfection of my own body.

As I watch, the *Voice* echoes in my ears and reminds me of the excitement I feel at being made of pure rubber. It reminds me that many men yearn to have a rubber skin that contains and defines them as mine does. It tells me that men sometimes come to my Master to beg to be given such a perfect rubber skin.

It tells me that some men even beg Him to change them into a robot such as I…

————————

The images flash upon the screen.

They show the now rubber-skinned young man over several days.

Sometimes he lies upon the workbench, with tubes and instruments inserted into his body.

The Rubberman moves around him. As he works the equipment hums and clicks, recording details of his captive's brainwave patterns and physiological status. Sometimes the computers seem to be feeding this data back into the young man as the Rubberman records his responses…

The camera sometimes shows the Rubberman merely standing by the young man's head, gloved hand gently stroking his bald head in a gesture of possessive protection. He talks quietly to the prone figure and seems to be repeating the same phrases over and over. The young man seems to relax under the Rubberman's touch. It seems as though he yearns for these quiet moments…

————————

The images flash, and the camera shows the Rubberman stroking the beautiful black-skinned body – applying a glossy polish to the already shining rubber form. At his touch, the young man's cock becomes hard. His body does not move, but moans and gasps escape his rubbered lips. The Rubberman seems pleased with this reaction, and begins to stroke and tease the young man more. As his gloved hands glide over the smooth rubber skin, he tells him what a good boy he is – how much he loves the touch of his Master upon his rubber skin.

At his words, the young man twitches and moans even more.

The Rubberman strokes the shiny black cock and balls – his other gloved hand moving over the naked body: stroking, touching, teasing…

Finally, the Rubberman gives a spoken command: the young man's back arches in pleasure and thick cum oozes out of the black dildo that is now his cock. He seems to cum over and over – each spurt accompanied by another shuddering moan of ecstasy.

The white cum is stark and beautiful against the glossy black of his skin.

Finally the Rubberman scoops up some of the spent cum in his rubber-gloved hand. The young man sucks it eagerly from the gloved fingers. The act of having his own cum fed back to him seems to excite both the young man and the Rubberman a great deal.

The instruments and machines impassively record every moment…

————

The images continue to flash.

Each time they show the young man he appears less and less human.

His movements are slower now, less organic – the layers of rubber that coat his flesh make him stiff and he cannot move as easily as he could before.

His eyes are the only part that shows that he is still human – dark brown, they stare blankly out of the anonymously smooth rubber mask that is now his face…

Sometimes the young man stands before a mirror. His movements are sluggish, drugged – but his eyes shine. His hands caress his body: exploring his new rubber-flesh. His eyes burn hungrily from the blank mask – greedily, they take in every inch of rubber. His tongue licks his lips, tasting the rubber that coats them.

Sometimes he raises his hands before him – stares at them unbelieving. He sniffs the rubbered palms as he cups them over his nose, and then slowly licks along each smooth and glossy finger. You can hear his moans as he does so… His rubber lips move as he repeats to himself over and over: "*It's really happening – I really am rubber – He is transforming me into a rubber-droid!*"…

The camera focuses on the young man's face. It shows the overwhelming excitement that shines in his eyes as he repeats these words to himself…

As I lie on my Master's workbench and allow these images to complete their reprogramming, I find myself excited by the changes they show in this young man – excited as his human form transforms and becomes more like my own. More and more like a creation of my Master…

As I watch and am reprogrammed by the images and the *Voice*, I think of how much this young man would love to serve my Master. I even wonder if this young man might be one of the men the *Voice* tells me about – men like those that I have seen at the clubs that Master sometimes takes me to. The men who stand and watch as I serve my Master, and obey His every command without question…

The men who stare hungrily as my body morphs and changes to His command…

The men whom the *Voice* tells me envy my own enslaved state.

The men who beg my Master to change them and transform them – mutate and assimilate their bodies and minds to become androids like myself…

————

The images flash. They end with a full body shot of the young man.

He is completely hairless.

His skin is covered in a perfect, seamless rubber coating.

His body shines glossy black under the lights.

He seems more muscular now: the rubber that coats him also restricts him. The tension defines his muscles and makes his body perfect. The blackness draws the eye…

These differences are subtle, but as the camera focuses in it is clear that there is one major change: before, the dark brown eyes were all that remained of his humanity – burning with hunger within the impassive mask of his rubber face – but now, those brown eyes are lost behind the unblinking stare of contact lenses. Their silvered surfaces reflect his distorted self-image back to him from the mirrors that line the room. He looks in vain for any sign of his earlier identity: all he can see is this pure rubber form. Nothing now remains of his humanity…

The images flash and the camera pans back.

Seated in a chair is the Rubberman. He watches the rubber-skinned being before him. His eyes shine within his own mask. There is a look of pride and ownership there.

He speaks to his creation and his masterpiece:

"*Who are you, boy?*"

The creature stands before the mirror – its blank shining eyes reflect back the glossy image of its rubber body…

The camera focuses upon the rubber creature's face. As it does so, the image is joined by a live feed of my own body: lying upon my Master's workbench and surrounded by the instruments that are re-programming me to be His perfect droid and slave…

The twin cameras zoom in until our two faces are overlaid – one over the other.

There is a perfect match.

For a moment I feel a lurch of realisation – a flash of pure excitement as I realise the truth of what I have seen. There is a brief instant where I am allowed to remember *everything* that my Master has done for me in granting my begged wish to become His droid…

Then all I feel is a wash of intense orgasmic pleasure as the programming is completed and I once more submit completely – *willingly* – to my Master's command.

Our lips move in unison, overlaid upon the screen, as both the transformed young man and I repeat the same words. They are the words of our programming – the words that have become our only Truth:

"*I am a rubber-droid.*
I am the property and pet of my Master:
He created and programmed me to serve and pleasure Him.

I exist to serve and obey only Him:
every touch or word from Him fills my being with pleasure.

I owe everything to my Master:
He created my rubber-body and programmed my mind.
Everything I need, want or desire comes from my Master.

I surrender everything to my Creator.
I am a bio-engineered creature of pure rubber.
My entire body – bones, skin, and teeth – is made of pure rubber.
I am naked and hairless.
My skin is coated in shiny, black, pliant rubber.

My robotic mind is empty and receptive to His commands.

I am a rubber-droid.
I am the property and pet of my Master:
He created and programmed me to serve and pleasure Him…"

*"…purely and only His possession: played with
and used, then cleaned and stored away…"*

Rubber-worm

There is a rubber-themed calendar on my bedroom wall. Each month features a different horny guy in various forms of rubber – but it is 'Mr October' that fascinates me the most…

He is dressed in a rubber butcher's apron, mask and boots – and there's just something so medical, bestial, and decidedly *perverted* about that image: his broad shoulders and rippling muscles emphasised by the long shining rubber apron, his hands enfolded in thick heavy gloves and his powerful thighs encased in waders.

He is part butcher, part doctor, part mad scientist – and his cold eyes stare over the mask. Beneath that steely gaze, I feel myself reduced to a piece of meat to be operated upon, tested, and adapted – and my cock stirs with perverse hunger.

I imagine Him towering over me: my rubber-clad Master looking down at my rubbered and squirming body. I feel myself yielding to that cold stare – and with a shudder, I slip under His control and the black pull of the rubber…

I feel Him as He draws me down into His liar – forces my weakening body down onto the cold-steel table. He straps me down and plants an IV through the rubber that coats my arm… I feel the cold spread through my skin as He pumps a cocktail of psychotropics and steroids into my bloodstream – and hear myself groan as reality slips away from me under the influence of the drugs. He lifts my head, and encases it into a VR helmet – then uses it to pump porn and subliminal messages into my befuddled brain.

The drugs, the rubber, and the hypnosis start to blur the edges between reality and fantasy, humanity and porn…

Strapped-down, rubber-encased, helplessly turned on, I feel myself start to slip away. My slack mouth drools into the hood as I feel myself slowly surrendering to the hypnosis – staring with blank empty eyes as the perversion pumps deeper and deeper into me, pushes me further and further from any sense of reality or self or humanity – filling my brain with only lust and depravity and bestial need…

Under its influence, I feel the rubber come alive: squirming over my helpless writhing body, seeping through my pores, worming into my mouth and arse and piss-slit – pulsing into every cavity, and filling me up… My body throbs with pain and perverse hunger as my eyes are covered, filled in, glossed over: become hollow, blank, and empty. My mouth stretches wide in a silent scream – but the rubber-tide rises up and over my lips, pulsing down into my throat – filling my stomach and guts and core…

My whole face slowly disappears into an unrecognisable blob of rubber that moves and ripples. My body becomes only a seething mass of glossy black as glistening liquid rubber flows over my limbs, coating them in layer after layer until they become heavy and stiff; thick layers of slick blackness mound and mould into rubberised muscle until my body twitches and grunts with animal need.

Within this mutating body, my mind is assaulted on every side: programmed deeper and deeper into pure and empty service for the

Man who controls the whole process – the rubber-genius who works the machines that convert me, and who watches my dehumanisation from the shadows…

His cold eyes watch as the process mutates my body ever further into little more than a rubber-encased object – a tireless rubber-toy devoted only to the pleasure of the perverted mind that has taken and transformed me. All identity and individuality removed – lost beneath the glossy rubber layers and utterly separated from humanity: no identity, no history, no face but the rubber that encases and transforms me into a dehumanised object for my Master's pleasure…

And like a true pervert, I find myself utterly and deeply aroused by this thought…

But the Master continues to push and tweak – perverting me ever deeper.

He pumps my body with yet more drugs, coats it ever thicker in rubber – until my swollen, muscular limbs press together so tightly that they start to merge and my body regresses. The rubber, muscle, and flesh blending as one as the creature that I have become mutates into a seething, writhing mass of rubber and mindless desire…

My body and mind is now so utterly changed that it has regressed to a worm-like state: I have become only a rippling tube of formless rubber-muscle – my face a smooth curve of rubber, my throat and arse a slick rippling tube, ready and eager to be filled and fucked and pissed into.

My Master releases me from my bonds, and my pumped and swollen body flops to the floor. Barely able to move, I wriggle and slop across the ground. Little more than a rubber-slug, I hump along a lube-slick trail of my own leaking juices – blind head seeking out the scent of my Master – moaning and gurgling with subhuman hunger as I try to find my place at His boots…

My altered and unrecognisable body glistens with pre-cum that oozes from every rubberised pore. My skin shivers with pleasure as I finally reach His feet, and feel the touch of His waders upon my now blind face. I feel my throat open wide, dripping with saliva as I helplessly moan in hunger and desire – wordlessly beg my Maker to use me and feed my perverted body with His juices…

He probes my gaping mouth with His gloved hand – sneers at the sucking, choking sounds I make as He slowly forces His fist down my undulating throat – testing me, preparing me – imagining how it will feel to slide His cock into this willing rubber hole…

He is pleased with Himself – proud of how His power has taken a man and transformed him into a greedy, rubberised worm: coiled at His boots and hungry only to serve Him. A warm, soft, slick, wet rubber-hole and nothing more. Proud of how He has transformed this man into a perfect rubber fuck-tube, fit only for Him to dump His fluids into – a creature that greedily sucks at Him with grunts and squeals and animal sounds – incapable of anything but mindless worship of the Master who has so completely warped its body and mind to His service…

———

I find myself lost in the perversity of these darkly self-destructive thoughts – and the lure of being so utterly surrendered to my fetish that I finally and completely become nothing more than an object – my Master's kinky possession.

Devoid of any humanity or consciousness: His beautifully depraved creature.

Transformed by my Master into His mindless rubber-toy – little more than a dildo or jack-tube, and no more important to Him than His waders. A dehumanised object to be used for His pleasure, then stored away with His gear.

My rubberised body harnessed and hung up amidst His leather and rubber – connected to pumps and pipes that sustain my limited rubberised life and consciousness until He has need of me. A beautifully glossy black object: mute, blind and senseless – capable of making no demands, nor refusing any order – but equally, unrestricted by any physical limitation or ethical concern – and so finally free to perform any sexual service that He could ever wish for.

Finally and completely surrendered to my fetish and obsessions – become purely and only His possession: played with and used, then cleaned and stored away – aware of nothing but the vague passing of time before I am taken out again to be pumped and fucked and used once more…

*"…He showed me that some Men actually like their
boys to be lightweight and easy to lug around…"*

"And that was when the police burst in…"

There are times when our fantasy lives collide with reality. Sometimes those moments can be frightful and dangerous, but they can also be intensely cathartic. Occasionally we can even look back on them and laugh – as anyone who has their own 'Coming out' story will know.

The experience I want to share took place back when I was still new to bondage and BDSM.

I was still very uncertain of myself, and hugely self-conscious about being short, skinny and very inexperienced – but a wonderful Bondage Top in London took me in His gauntleted hands, and showed me that some Men actually *like* their boys to be lightweight and easy to lug around…

He was an intense Top, but a complete gentleman, and I was honoured to make several visits to Him over the years. He took me to my first fetish club – leathered and collared, kneeling by His side in the Hoist in London. Eyes wide and amazed at the play I saw on display there.… He carefully watched over me through-out my first night spent in full rubber encasement and bondage – guiding me towards my longed for rubber-surrender with understanding and gentleness. It was He who gave me my first 'flight' in suspension – and also my first experience of electro... He even gave me my first pair of leather chaps.

Best of all, He took time to build an incredible level of trust between us – and it was that which enabled me to surrender to Him without fear. That slowly built level of complete trust between us also enabled Him to take me – *US!* – on some of the most intense and pleasurable bondage experiences either of us has ever had.

————

The incident in question was one of the last visits I was able to make with Him.

I had previously confessed to a fantasy of being kidnapped and forced into complete rubber-surrender – and so I was thrilled when He gave me my orders: When I arrived at the station, I was not to try to find Him on the platform; instead, I was to leave by one of the quieter side exits...

As I walked through the archway, I felt a gloved hand grab my shoulder and arm. A man's deep, rough voice told me to keep my face down, and he half led, half pushed me down an alley to a parked white van. My captor told me to stand still then, whilst my wrists where handcuffed and a heavy leather blackout hood was pulled over my head – then I was put into the back of the van and my ankles tied.

My 'Kidnapper' made a few checks to make sure I was safely restrained, and then drove off with me bumping and groaning in the back...

When we stopped, I was hustled out of the van and into a house – still hooded and cuffed, and loving the disorientation and the rush of adrenaline-edged fear I was feeling.

Safely inside, my hands were un-cuffed, and I was told to strip out of my leather – revealing my hidden rubber skin as I did so. I was ordered to close my eyes, and the hood was carefully removed – only to be replaced by a rubber hood, head-harness, and blindfold. A chest harness and restraints where then placed upon me, and they were used to fasten me against the wall with my feet spread and my arms strapped behind me: exposed and helpless – and still unable to see who had captured me or where I was.

Through it all, I could hear low voices and the sound of a camera – and so I knew that there was more than one person present, and that my predicament was being recorded…

I was left in the dark to consider my fate for a while.

At one point, I was sure that I heard heavy knocking at the front door, and I could hear voices whispering *"ignore it – it'll be kids messing about"* – but I thought nothing of it…

After a while, my Captor came back; a poppers soaked cloth was held over my gagged mouth and I was forced to take a big hit – sagging into the restraints as the buzz hit me and my head swam. Then, out of the dizzying darkness, there were hands upon me: touching, exploring, probing, and testing – with the rubber and the poppers heightening every touch…

They finally removed me from the wall. I was forced to bend over and I felt something hard against the front of my neck – my hands where pulled in front of me and rested on the same surface whilst my booted feet where pushed apart. As the locking bars trapped my neck, wrists and ankles I realised I was restrained within a set of wooden stocks.

With my body helpless, my captor took advantage of my exposed arse: using various leather straps and canes to beat me harder and harder until I was sobbing into the darkness of my hood and desperately trying to pull away.

And then he strapped me a little bit more – just to make it clear who was now in control.

I had never felt so utterly helpless – or so turned on.

I was left to recover for a moment, and then I was released from the stocks.

A hand grabbed my collar: forcibly pulled me into the centre of the room, and then pushed me down onto my knees. A funnel was pushed into the gag: the bitter taste of piss filled my mouth, and I was forced to swallow or choke.

All the while, the camera clicked away beside and behind me – recording my humiliation.

I was pulled to my feet again – then man-handled over to a low bench and forced to lie down; there was some adjusting, and then I could feel a sleepsack being zipped up and strapped down over my body: sealing me in tight and hard and utterly powerless.

A rubber sheet was pulled over my head – covering my eyes whilst the head-harness, gag, and blindfold were removed. A heavy hooded gasmask with blacked out lenses then replaced them. I felt the mask move as a breathing tube was screwed into the intake ports – and then another screwed into the end of that one – and then another – tube after tube in an ever lengthening corrugation that snaked across my bound and rubbered body. Each new tube only made it harder and harder to breathe – until I could feel the gasmask sucking tight to my face with each struggling breath as I fought against the rubber restraints and the tightness of the sleepsack – and my own rising panic…

Just as I was starting to feel the buzz of true asphyxia, I finally felt most of the tubes removed – and was suddenly breathing easier again. I panted in huge moaning breaths – and only realised that the air was heavily laced with pure poppers when my head began to thump and the blackness of my vision began to sparkle with lights…

Still reeling from the poppers, I felt a large capacity rebreathing bag being screwed into the tube and placed on my chest, so that I would be able to feel it swell and deflate with each ragged breath. Just as I was getting to the point of hypoxia, I was allowed a few clean breaths – and then forced to take another deep hit of poppers before the bag was reapplied. Then I was left to pant and struggle once more.

It was then that he pulled down the zipper on the sack and strapped an electro-sex unit onto my cock and balls…

I was in rubber-piggy heaven: defeated by this demonstration of my Master's total control and my complete powerless: all resistance and thought wiped clean by asphyxia and heavy poppers – and loving every moment.

I was so high that I swear I even had an out of the body experience at one point…

––––––––

Unfortunately, it was at this moment – just as things were getting interesting – that the hammering at the door *really* started in earnest.

I was left alone for a moment whilst my Captor went to see what the noise was about. Through the muffling darkness of the hood, I could just about hear someone ask:

"Who is it…?"

Then a very loud and very frightening voice called out:

"This is the police – open this door NOW or we will break it down…!"

At first, I thought it was joke – but the feeling of panic in the room was all too real – as was the sound of the door crashing open and several police officers bursting into my Captor's front room…

I heard them starting to question him about who else was present in the house. The other guy in the playroom was called into the other room – and then I had to lie there – still bound, still hooded, but trying to be completely silent – whilst they were both interrogated.

A cold weight of fear settled in my stomach, as they were told that a woman had seen a young man being bundled into a van outside the train station. She had taken the registration and phoned the police, fearing for this young man's life. The police had tracked the van's license to this address, and they now wanted to know if either of them knew anything about an attempted kidnap…

I lay there, heart sinking, and thought of my family and friends, still unaware of my fetish – and I thought of their shame when the story broke in the papers: of me found fully rubbered, helpless, bound – and at the centre of a police raid…!

I could hear my Top trying to prevaricate: asking to see warrant cards and clarifying what he was being accused of – and then my heart sank as I heard one of the officers asking what was in the other room.

There was the sound of heavy boots stomping up the hallway; the door opened. There was a horrible moment of silence, and then:

"Sarge – you'd better get in here: it looks like they've got some poor kid strapped up in a rubber sack!"

I heard them ordering my Top back into the room.

He was commanded to remove my hood – and then I was blinking under bright lights and looking up at three huge police officers and their sergeant – all in security gear and high-vis and looking *very* disturbed and angry…!

They demanded to know who I was, and my Top tried to answer that I was just a friend – but they cut Him off and demanded that I speak for myself.

That has *got* to be one of the weirdest moments in my life: bound tight on the floor in a rubber sleepsack – my head throbbing from poppers and BC, pickling in my own cooling sweat and piss – and looking up at four genuine police officers…

Desperately, I tried to keep my adrenaline hard-on under control – and to appear perfectly happy and at ease. I calmly thanked my Top for taking off my hood – I could see he was shaking, and so I ignored the officers for a moment to ask if He was OK…

Then, I looked up at these huge and scary man, and very politely (and in my best University educated voice), I tried to explain that *these were my very good friends, and that we were simply playing a few games together. Whilst I was thankful for their obvious concern, I was in fact perfectly well, and very happy. That, despite appearances, I had actually asked to be helped into the rubber sack in which I was now lying – and that it was in fact quite a pleasant experience… And, yes, my family and friends knew where I was, and who I was with. But, really, it was all just a *terrible* misunderstanding – I certainly hadn't been 'bundled' anywhere, and I couldn't imagine why the poor old lady could have thought that I was being harmed at all – maybe it had just been a little dark and she had been mistaken in thinking I was being put into the back of the van…?! I did hope that she was OK – but that really, no one needed to be overly worried at all!*

(It is also how I know that I am a pervert: because even through the panic and fear, there was still a small part of me that was excitedly checking out their riot gear and boots…)

I guess my persuasive powers must have worked: because they checked over a few details and addresses and then finally agreed that everything seemed to be OK…! Amazingly, they left my Top with only a verbal caution – and the suggestion that any 'games' should be kept out of the public view in future.

Needless to say we didn't continue with the scene after they left: we were all too shaken up, and my Top was understandably in a terrible state… But we did have a good laugh about it the next morning – after we had time to calm down…

He later told me that He has never tried to repeat the scene – and finds that even the idea of kidnapping someone now gives Him palpitations… It is a shame, because it was building into one of the hottest scenes we had done to that point.

The other sad thing was that the other guy had desperately destroyed the film in his camera as soon as he knew what was going on, so we also lost all of the photos too.

Still, it was one hell of an experience – and quite funny now I have the distance to look back on it. God knows what those poor police officers thought about it!

Interestingly: I have never been able to look at a UK police officer or a High-Vis jacket in quite the same way since…

"…My mouth is suddenly dry as I hover for a moment over the smooth thick leather…"

Bound

Early morning: 8am on a weekday. I'm on my own and enjoying some 'me-time': an hour or so between my partner leaving for work and me having to do the same…

Of course, that means I'm lying back on the bed, giving my sore muscles a bit of a rub after my daily exercise – and my rubber-covered crotch a bit of a rub too…

I have a small home gym, so I love to do my work-outs rubbered up. It's not normally anything too full-coverage or restrictive: just enough to feel the rubber without it getting in the way too much… I've got a great pair of really tight, pouch-fronted shorts that are my favourite work-out gear: they keep my cock and arse tight, rubbered and wet – and my appetite perked – but they don't really interfere with the real business of trying to keep my hard-gainer body that little bit trim and buffed. There are occasions when I also slip on a T-shirt – and maybe my chaps – but that always leads to a gradual layering as each piece of rubber merely builds my hunger for more – until I'm creaking about under every item of rubber I possess – including hood and gasmask…

I really try to save that for days when I know that I have the time to let go to the full rubber experience…

So instead, here I am, relaxing a little and getting my breath back: one hand rubbing my chest and playing with my nipple ring, the other gently kneading my stiffening cock through the rubber…

I am just thinking about getting out my thick rubber gloves when I'm disturbed by the ring of the doorbell…

Damn – the bloody postman!

It is probably another plain-wrapped catalogue from Invincible or Wet-Hot Rubber… So I lever myself off the bed, pull on my army fatigues and a hoodie and head down the stairs…

I don't see the familiar brown uniform of the UPS man as I peer through the spy-hole – instead I'm met with the glossy shine of a motorcycle helmet and the blank stare of a darkened visor… My curiosity is piqued, and I open the door – not thinking to put the safety chain on first…

I have a moment to get an impression of a tall man: black leather one-piece and silver-plated motto-cross boots – then he is upon me: quick, fast and quiet. One hand grabs my wrist and pushes it up behind my back, the other clamps itself over my mouth. I taste and smell the thick leather of his gauntlets – and despite myself, my cock twitches in its tight rubber prison…

He leans forward. I see my own startled face reflected in his visor, and behind it, the impression of intense eyes. They hold me in place as thoroughly as his gloved hand. His voice is muffled but clear:

"*Make a noise and you'll regret it. Keep quiet, do as you're told, and you might just find you enjoy this*"

For a moment my mind races – fear, apprehension, worry – but my stiffening cock floods my mind and clouds my reason and I find myself giving one uncertain nod.

"Good – now, slowly and quietly, back up."

He pushes me backwards into the hallway, uses one booted foot to close the door behind him…

The light reflects off his helmet as he nods behind me and to his right:

"That the Kitchen?"

Again, I find myself nodding.

"Good – back-up into there then, boy"

We shuffle backwards. In my heightened state I am aware of everything: the creak of his leathers, the click of his boots as they find the tiled kitchen floor, my own stifled breathing muffled by the warm gauntlet that is still clamped over my mouth and nose – and the intensifying ache of my cock as it twitches and struggles under its secret layers of rubber…

He pushes me into the middle of the room, and then stops… Once more, I'm caught in the steady gaze of those barely seen eyes…

"Now boy – I'm going to take away my hand for a moment – you make one sound and all of this over. Do you understand?"

Quicker this time, I nod.

He lifts his hand off slowly – waiting to see what I do. I keep my mouth shut and my eyes riveted on his…

"Good lad"

One hand still holding my arm, he unzips a jacket pocket and pulls out a pair of steel handcuffs. They glint for a moment as he looks at me – there is a challenge in that pause.

Slowly, uncertainly, I respond to his unspoken demand: move my free arm behind my back…

He reaches around me and I feel the click of cold steel around my wrists. I feel my cock react instantly to my complicity – and with a shudder that shakes my body, something deep inside me melts…

He must have felt it – and known what it meant – for in that moment he steps closer. His arms enclose my shoulders and slowly, quietly, he pulls me into the leathered warmth of his body… Instinctively, unconsciously, my head sinks to the leather of his chest – and he responds to my implicit surrender with a tightening embrace and a deep soothing growl.

We stand like that for a moment as he lets my submission wash over me – then:

"OK – on your knees, boy"

Quietly I sink to my knees, my head bowed. I fix my gaze onto the steel toe of his beautiful boots.

I hear what sounds like a chuckle:

"Good. Now: Sit! Stay!"

His boots move out of my view and I hear him opening the front door again. He is gone for a few moments, and then I hear him close and lock the front door behind him…

His boots come back into my view, and a large black bag thumps onto the floor beside them.

I hear a jingle as my house-keys go into his jacket, and he zips the pocket closed…

"Now lad – some rules.

From now on, you are simply "boy." You will find you won't have much opportunity to speak, but you are to think of me simply as "SIR".

For the next 4 hours, you are mine and you will do everything I tell you. You will not be expected to express an opinion or make requests – I already know everything I need to about you: every limit and boundary, every fantasy, fetish, and desire.

If you obey, and do as you are told, I will not hurt or damage you – but resist or disobey me, and you will suffer the consequences…

Do you understand, boy?"

My mind is racing – what does he mean, he knows everything he needs to about me? Who is this guy?! But my cock does my thinking for me once more, and I find myself whispering:

"Yes SIR!"

"Good boy"

He steps toward me again, and his boots fill my field of vision

"Go on boy – show 'em the respect they deserve!"

Hands still cuffed behind me, I shuffle awkwardly towards him, lean forward. My mouth is suddenly dry as I hover for a moment over the smooth thick leather – taking them in… I lean further – almost fall onto his boots – press my mouth to the toe in one deep kiss. The smell of boot-oil and polish is strong and pungent: it fits like a key into the submissive part of my mind and unlocks the boot-pig inside me… With a groan, I push my bearded face into the leather and start to make love to Sir's boots…

Lost in the smell and the feel of his boots, I am also lost to the time – and to myself. I have no idea how long I have been there on the floor at his feet, but my face is wet with my own saliva, smudged and smeared with polish. I am distantly aware that I am grunting and moaning. My hips slowly grinding as I work my tongue over first one boot and then the other. I hear his encouraging growl and feel his gloved hand rubbing the back of my head and neck. I feel myself respond: moaning louder and rubbing my face over the instep of his boot. I hear his leather creak as he leans back against the wall, and then his gloved hand is replaced by the sole of his other boot. I feel the rubber cleats as they press down into my neck: pushing me further down into the leather and into my piggish headspace…

"Yeah – that's it boy – that's my little boot-pig – my hot little boot-brush"

There's a distant part of me that is shocked at hearing that phrase – in hearing that name: *bootbrush*… a part that wonders if there is a conscious use of the name given me by my partner and Top… But it's a distant part – and one easily overridden by the boot-pig that I have become…

"OK boy – enough"

He slips a boot under me and then pushes me off with a boot in my chest… I sit back on my heels, panting – oblivious to the drooling state I am in…

"Right – time to see what else I've got"

He moves closer again. He leans over me, reaches down to unlock and remove the handcuffs from my wrists. Released, I instinctively lean into the leather warmth of his legs…

He reaches into another pocket. Even before he pulls it out, I hear the distinctive rattle of a dog's choke chain…

Knowing what comes next, I bow my head further – offer him my bare neck… I feel a shiver pass through me at the touch of the cold metal, and give a deep sexual grunt at the 'click' of the padlock as it locks me in…

Out of another pocket comes a chain dog-leash with a leather handle. The padlock bumps against my chest as he clicks the links together.

His hand lingers for a moment, resting on the back of my head…

"Now: heel!"

I make to rise to my feet – but his hand stops me, pushes me back down – keeps pushing me forward onto my hands and knees…

*"No, pup – I said '**HEEL**!'"*

He gives the leash a sharp tug, and I am forced to follow him on all fours.

He walks us out of the kitchen and turns to the stairs. I struggle to stay close to his legs as I clamber up the narrow hallway. The padlock feels like a strangely familiar weight and the chain is tight around my neck. Although walking on all fours should be difficult, it somehow seems almost natural – and I find myself falling into a more dog-like state of mind. I feel my world shrink and focus onto his hand were it holds the leash: I swear that the tangy scent of his leather glove is more intense in this state.

I feel my tongue hang out as I pant around the restriction of the collar as he pulls me up the stairs and into the bedroom. I follow him on all fours and feel my head hang in shame as the heady scent of my piled rubber gear brings me back to myself with a snap…

"Well, looks like I've got myself a little rubber-pup, eh?"

I settle back onto my haunches and stare at the floor in front of his boots. I feel my face flush in guilt and shame…

"No need for that pup – there's nothing here to be ashamed of…"

I feel his gloved hand cup my chin, and realise that at some point he must have lost his 'lid', because I find myself gazing into a heavily moustached face and intense hazel eyes.

"It looks like everything I heard about you was true, pup – I think that we're both going to enjoy your time with me, little doggie!"

He stares into my eyes – I see strength and control there, but also passion and humour – I feel myself fall into that intense gaze, opening up to it and the power that it represents… Then the spell is broken as he smiles and ruffles my hair…

"Time to get you more appropriately dressed, boy"

He reaches down to my neck and unlocks the leash from my collar;

"On your feet boy: strip"

Trembling, I climb to my feet. I try to ignore the cramp in my legs.

Slowly, carefully, I pull off my hoodie and let my army fatigues slide to the floor. I pick them up, turn, and quietly fold them onto the bedside chair. I realise that this will be the first time he gets to see the inked lines that cover my back, chest, and arms.

My crotch is a hard bulge in the pouched front of my rubber shorts… I move to slide these off too – but he shakes his head:

"They can stay on boy – for now it's your head I intend to play with…"

I place my bare feet shoulder-width apart, square my shoulders and put my hands behind my back. With my head up, but my eyes fixed to the floor in front of his feet, I stand proud yet submissive – open to his gaze and awaiting his orders.

He stands and watches me for a moment – then he moves closer… His hands move quietly over my body: feeling, probing, testing – I am simply aware of the warmth of his body, the strength of his hands, the possession in his gaze…

A finger traces the tattooed line of a branch that curves over my shoulder and onto my chest. It briefly stops over my heart, where an inked chain and dog-tag glints amongst the tattooed leaves. I wonder if he can make out the word 'bootbrush' permanently marked there – and then feel a wash of pride as I hear his appreciative *"Nice touch!"*

He seems pleased with what he sees.

With a hand on my shoulder he gives the quiet command *"Stay!"* and then goes downstairs to retrieve his bag.

When he returns, he drops the bag onto the side of the bed and starts pulling things out of it: rope, chains, blindfolds… He places them all carefully to one side on the bed – and then I hear a distinctive squeak and rustle as he straightens and turns to me, his hands holding what I think at first is a folded rubber sheet…

My eyes widen when he lets the rubber unfold so that I can finally see what it is that he holds: a thick rubber sleepsack, with the smooth nub of an attached hood, and zippers at crotch, arse and tits…

He smiles:

"Welcome to your home for the day!"

He smiles even more when my cock visibly kicks inside my rubber shorts…

It is now much later – but I have no idea how much later. It could be hours – or even days. A distant part of me wonders if it has been long enough for my partner to have returned from work, and wonder where I am…

I am lost in a dark, wet world of sensory deprivation and sexual overload – my body held in the inescapable tight embrace of thick rubber. My hands are sealed into rubberised balls and my arms pinned to my sides in thick internal sleeves; heavy leather straps bind my body at strategic points, making me incapable of much movement beyond a desperate wriggle… But even when I can find space to move, the rubber simply gives and stretches a little, then snaps my body back into hungry submission.

Thick rubber covers my face, fills my mouth, stuffs my nose and blinds my eyes… Through the heavy rubber, I can just feel the headphones that alternately – randomly – feed me music, hypnotic tapes and my Sir's voice – or the amplified sounds of my own struggling to be free…

My only other link to the outside is the breathing tube – snaking away from the hooded gasmask that is padlocked tight around my neck, completing my cocooned form. The tube through which I have been fed poppers and my Sir's own breath. The tube that is occasionally blocked or restricted so that I have to writhe and struggle to breathe…

My breathing is restricted once more – I feel the gasmask clamp itself to my face as I desperately try to draw air into myself – struggle and gasp and writhe in panic. Bound and breathless, I cannot help but fight against the imprisoning rubber – and the darkness that threatens to engulf me. But even as I struggle, I feel my tortured cock stiffen with asphyxia and pump yet another load into the rubber sheath that already holds the slimy remains of countless others…

Spent, exhausted, totally helpless, I feel myself sink back. I hear the headphones switch back from my own grunting cries to the soothing sounds of the hypnotic tape that tells me to relax, to let go, to sleep…

I know that I will have a short while to recoup – a few moments to slip into that half-sleep where the tape and the enclosure can do its work in loosening my mind and breaking my spirit. But I also know that I will be shortly awoken once more to the slowly building tingle of the TENS unit at my cock, balls, and tits. Awoken to the start of another round of slowly building arousal, but not knowing if this time it will end in gasping release like the last – or in hours of frustration as I am kept teetering on the brink, only to be left unsatisfied…

I feel the bed move – and in the fug and confusion of my encapsulated body, I realise that it is Sir back again. I tense for a moment and then feel myself instinctively relax as I feel the possessive touch of his hand through the rubber sack… and then I feel a rush of confused emotions – relief, disappointment, and hope – as I feel the collar unlocked from around my neck and the gasmask slowly removed.

I hear his voice again:

"Keep your eyes closed for a moment…"

Then his hands roll me onto my side. I feel him carefully undoing the laces on the hood, then pulling down the long zip. Slowly my head is released from its tight rubber prison. The cold of the air against my face tells me that I am bathed in sweat…

It is still dark, and I realise that he must have turned off the lights so as not to blind my dark-adapted eyes.

I feel his hand stroke my face – and then he tells me to open my eyes…

And find myself staring into the face and eyes of my partner!

Confused, I turn my head – to find the man I have been thinking of as 'Sir' standing on the other side of the bed. I look between them, my confusion evident on my face. Seeing my look, my partner laughs and ruffles my sweat-damp hair:

"Yes brush – I've been here for the last 2 hours – watching, helping, enjoying… That last time: that was me"

"But…." I manage to stammer, as 'Sir' swings onto the bed beside us. My partner drapes a hand over my crotch and grins over my still bound form.

"You're not the only one with contacts, sweetheart! I knew you had a fantasy for a scene like this – and that you'd only resist the idea of setting it up for yourself – and so I thought I'd make a little arrangement that would suit us both. You get to live out a major fantasy of being 'kidnapped' by a mysterious Master and turned into his helplessly bound rubber-slug, and I get to watch and join in – all without your knowledge! And 'Rubber-Biker' here was only too happy to oblige – seeing as he got to play with my hot bit of property in the process…"

"And he was everything that you promised too – my respects to you: you've trained yourself one filthy rubber pup here!"

The two men share a look over my restrained body – then 'Rubber-biker' grins, and my partner pulls him over me and into a deep kiss.

Lying bound beneath them I can't help but grunt at the sight of these two heavily bearded men trading tongues!

They both look down at me:

"Looks like the grub might be ready for some more…?"

"Sir, yes Sirs!!"

*"…he moves and thinks so much like a real
dog, tail wagging in pleasure…"*

Dog-napped

Evening

8pm on a Friday in late September.

Shit, I hate working this late evening – it really fouls up my weekend!

Nevertheless, I do the right thing and put on a smile for my colleague as we clear the last person out of the Library building. Finally, the long day is over, as we lock the door and I head for my office.

My computer hums to itself in the darkness. Before shutting down, I make one last check of my e-mail to see if any of the guys from IRC have sent me anything. There are not many perks to being a librarian in a conservative town, but that's the one thing that makes this job worthwhile: free access to the 'net and a private office!

I am not sure it is healthy for me though: I can sometimes spend hours on chat, losing myself in that virtual world of hot men and infinite possibilities. I have met several interesting guys there too – especially in #gayrubber, the main 'room' I hang out in. There's some really horny rubbermen in there with whom I've shared untold

fantasies, swapped pictures, and even dabbled in a little cyber-sex…
some I've even managed to meet 'in the flesh'…

As I scroll through my Inbox, I am hoping that one particular guy
might have replied to my last e-mail. I met him online a while ago and
thought his nic sounded really hot: Vulcanise. Wow, what images
that name conjured in my head! I have spent hours DCC-ing with
him over the last few weeks: swapping pics and ideas, confessing to
dark fantasies of transformation and rubber-transmutation. He is a
good-looking fucker: shaved head and goatee with eyes that seemed
to pierce through the screen and straight into my soul. Looked like a
meaty S.O.B. too: big and dominant and into transforming his boys
into mindless rubber slaves. Woof!

We talked for ages earlier this week. I know I ended up telling him far
too much: about feeling controlled by my obsession for rubber, about
liking dog-play, submission and mind-control – and about my dark
fantasy of being kidnapped on my way home from work, drugged and
imprisoned by a perverse Top who would take my body and mind and
transform me into his rubber-skinned creature.

I expected derision, but he only laughed and sent me one of his
favourite photos: a young man, four legged and horse-headed –
transformed into a rubber-pony. He told me that he liked the idea of
doing something similar to me – perhaps feeding into my naturally
puppy-like nature and transforming me into a rubber-dog…

That idea touched a button for both of us. I got rubbered-up and
wanked myself silly later that night to images of my body transformed
and coated in liquid rubber, identity and self mutated into something
completely other than I am – and loyally worshiping the man who had
effected that so longed for transformation…

We had exchanged e-mail addies and I later sent him the details of
my fetish homepage. I'd hoped the stories there might have inspired
him…

"No new messages on server".

Ah well – maybe after the weekend.

————

I pull on my much-loved and beat-up leather biker jacket, switch off the lights, and lock the main door behind me as I leave. Everyone else has gone – even the security guard will be checking the other side of the building. Sometimes I worry about leaving late like this: the streets are empty, quiet, and dark – anything could happen to me now and no one would even notice for hours.

I shudder, and then smile at how easy it is to spook myself.

The sky is dark and cloudy and it looks like rain: the nights are drawing in and autumn is finally here… I pull my jacket zipper up; seal myself into the tight warm embrace of leather. Only one car passes me as I start the long trudge home. Forgetting the busy day behind me, I allow myself to relax into the solitude of a long quiet walk…

I find my mind wandering to that e-mail again as I walk across the small junction of a dark street – barely noticing that the streetlight has gone again and the road is even darker than ever…

I am vaguely aware of movement from under a tree as I step back up onto the pavement. I have a momentary impression of a large man in bike leathers, his mirrored visor shining in the half-light as he lunges towards me.

Startled, I turn my back to him, step back into the street. I take a breath to shout, but he is too quick: a gauntleted hand closes itself over my open mouth, even as strong, vice-like arms wrap around my body. I take another muffled breath – in my panic, I am just aware of a strange sweet taste. I struggle as the leather fist clamps itself all the tighter to my nose and mouth. With each breath, the sweet smell seems to drain the life from my limbs. My head buzzes and I feel my knees start to buckle.

I feel myself folding into the arms that now support me, then nothing…

————

The next few hours are a hazy blur.

I am vaguely aware of sitting up in what I assume is the passenger seat of a car or van – I am not sure because my head is enclosed within a dark hood. My hands are cuffed together and I seem to be strapped into the seat in some way, which must have happened whilst I was still unconscious.

My head feels fuzzy and my mouth is dry. I try to swallow but my mouth is filled with the bitter leather of a pecker gag; I guess that it must be there to prevent me from swallowing my own tongue whilst I was unconscious. Maybe that is a good sign: the guy mustn't want me to choke to death or anything.

The vehicle we are in seems to be moving – at high speed from the sound and vibration of the engine. I guess we must be on a motorway from the steadiness of the drive. Through the leather of the hood, I can hear the driver beside me: and the creak of his wet leathers as he changes gear to overtake. I shift a little in my seat, and make a muffled grunt into the gag, hoping to attract his attention.

Nothing.

I am chilled by the realisation that there is nothing I can do. I am cuffed, hooded and strapped into a speeding vehicle – driven by a complete stranger and heading who knows where.

I should be terrified…

―――――――

I guess I must eventually have slept, because the next thing I know the engine noise is echoing back off the walls of what I assume must be an underground garage. From the muffled noise of road traffic coming from outside, I guess we must be in a big city…

The car swings into a parking space, and the engine is turned off – it rocks a little as the man climbs out. I feel the door beside open, and I tense in the seat. There is a moment of silence, then that leather glove closes itself over my gagged mouth again – the sweet smell hits me and I feel myself slip away once more…

I come awake to the realisation that I am now lying down on my side. I am still hooded and gagged, but leather straps have replaced the cuffs around my wrists, and now my ankles are also bound. The surface beneath me is coated in something that feels like thick padded rubber.

My cock twitches as I think of the very real possibility that I might just have been kidnapped, and that I am now lying helpless and bound within some-one's dungeon. I can only think of one person who might have done this to me. I'm still scared, but now I'm also incredibly excited. The two emotions fight each other in my head.

I am suddenly aware that I might not be alone. I strain to hear through the leather hood that encloses my head and seals me into this helpless darkness. I am not sure, but I think I might hear the slight creak of leather…

A hand reaches out of the darkness – touches my bound and helpless body; I twitch and shy away: frightened, unsure, and nervous. Excitement and anxiety combine and form a sick feeling in the pit of my stomach – and a burning ache deep inside me. A shudder travels through me as I feel the hand travel up my body, across my stomach and over my pecs – pulled taut by the leather and the ropes that hold my arms behind me…

A second hand reaches out, cups my crotch – twitching and straining against the denim. Through the hood I hear a deep chuckle: an appreciative sound. My cock leaps and strains even more…

The hand at my crotch stays were it is – cupping and caressing; the other roams around my bound form. This hand is strong, firm – remorseless as it explores my body: gently, firmly inspecting each limb, muscle and joint. Warmth spreads through me from its touch… and my fearful shudders slowly turn to shivers of excitement. Unbidden a moan escapes from around my gag and my crotch pushes itself into the warm cupped glove that holds it…

Another deep chuckle…

Then the hands remove themselves. My body feels cold without the warmth of their touch… Unconsciously I lean forward – trying to re-establish the connection – but nothing. Empty air and silence…

————

I am left in the dark for a while. Just long enough for my tightly secured limbs to begin to feel stiff and sore.

Then, movement:

A gentle hand lifts my hooded head, and then I feel my head and shoulders cushioned within a warm leathered lap.

The gag moves in my mouth: something slides through it and into me – I guess it is a straw… Uncertainly, cautiously, I suck upon it and cool liquid fills my mouth, dry and parched from the ether. Hungrily I suck the water into me, feel it fill me. Then I am only sucking air. I feel the tube being removed from the gag, and the hands gently lower my head back to the floor…

Gradually I feel warmth spread through me – a heaviness in my limbs, but different from the ether-numbness I felt before.

With the warmth comes a slowly building feeling of well being, even euphoria. Dimly I realise that the water might have been drugged in some way… I realise that I should be worried, but instead I feel happy, relaxed, safe…

I feel myself slowly sinking down into a warm dark space…

My body relaxed, my mind drifting, I feel myself lifted by strong arms. My bound torso slumps within his embrace and my head rests against a strong, powerful chest. Through the haze and the hood I can smell the powerful and heady scent of leather and male sweat; I moan a little and press my hooded face into the warmth and the hard flex of his muscle.

Then I am being set down – something soft and cushioned beneath me. Drugged, my limbs still wrapped in warmth and relaxation, I lie helpless but happy.

The strong hands move around my unresisting body: slowly but efficiently removing my clothes. The last piece to go is my shorts: a touch of cold steel sliding between the fabric and my bare skin, and then I feel them cut from me…

I now lie completely naked: stripped of everything except the hood that covers my head, and the restraints that bind my ankles and wrists…

Strong hands roam over my now naked body, stroke and caress my skin, run over the hair on my legs and chest… Fingers tug at the curls at my crotch… The hands move to my arms and legs – unclasp the restraints and then pull each limb to the corners of the cushioned bench beneath me. My relaxed muscles make no resistance, as I am bound, spread-eagled, and helpless: stretched wide and open to the gaze and touch of my captor…

His hands touch me. My body tingles as he massages warm oil into my skin: my cock twitches and swings in the air, and I shift in the bonds that hold me spread upon the couch.

I hear the sound of rhythmic scraping: sharp steel being sharpened against a leather strop.

I struggle a little more in panic. He places a hand upon my chest:

"Steady now, boy – I don't want to cut you…"

I lie still, and feel the cold sharp scrape of a straight razor on my chest as he begins to strip me of all the hair on my body – my chest, legs, and arms – even the hair under my pits… His hands work slowly, methodically… Where he has shaved, he also washes: the warm soapy water soothing on my cold skin.

Once he has shaved my front, he turns me over, re-attach the bonds – then the blade and the warm water move across my arse…

The air feels cool upon my naked skin as he turns me over once more and then moves away…

And so I lie: stretched out, bound and hooded and completely naked. I dimly realise that hours must have passed since I was first carried from the car, blind and helpless. In those hours, I have been stripped of my identity, my mind drugged and my body teased.

In those hours, I have also been slowly seduced to the point where my body now responds to the touch of my captor – yearns and hungers for Him…

Changes

Darkness. Silence.

Head encased, senses muffled and blind, overwhelmed by the smell of the leather hood that presses into my face. Body stretched and bound – open and exposed.

Every movement of the air ripples across my stripped and hairless, tingling skin – raises the hairs that are no longer there… Naked flesh hungers for the return of the gloved hands that have stripped and bound me – teased me with their caresses.

In my blinded state, I imagine every stir of the air to be His breath, warm upon my body… I find myself yearning, hungering for His attention again…

Within the enfolding darkness, I image I can hear a voice talking to me: telling me to relax, to let go – that everything is safe, everything is right – that the warmth is good, the warmth is right… I feel my body respond – feel it relax even further into the enfolding warmth…

The voice keeps murmuring within my mind – quiet and insistent. It tells me that it is good to let go, that it feels right to relax – to let my body do as the voice commands…. In the dark, warm place I now find myself within, I feel myself nod: it *does* feel good to let the voice take the tension away – to let the voice look after me…

…in the warmth and the dark the voice's quiet insistence and soft murmuring begin to feel the same as the warm hands did when they caressed my body… I feel myself respond to it as I did to the hands: unconsciously, and without thought…

…slowly, gradually, the voice becomes a part of me. It tells me how good I feel, and I realise that it is true: I *do* feel good – more relaxed than I ever have done before.

The voice tells me that all is well, that I can relax and let go – relax and let the warmth soak into me – relax and let the voice take over – relax, let go and sleep…

I drift away – caressed by the voice and soothed in the warm enfolding darkness.

My body forgotten, I feel as if I am floating in a dark and warm sea: weightless, motionless, without thought or concern. The voice whispers quietly in my head, and I sleep unawares…

––––––––

Warmth.

Darkness.

A slow, easy, relaxed pleasure.

And the Voice…

No time, no space.

No thought. No body. No mind.

There is only the Voice and the pleasure it gives…

The darkness is filled with a deep feeling of well-being: a knowledge that everything is OK – that everything is safe.

The Voice says it is so, and it is…

The Voice speaks: slowly the darkness recedes.

Thought returns – slow and sluggish in the warmth and the pleasure…

Awareness slowly grows and spreads: time, space, dimension… body, limbs, mouth… satellites all, basking in the bright warmth that is the Voice…

The Voice tells the body who and what it is: that it is a being with little thought or volition – a creature with no past or memory. The property and pet of the Voice…

The Voice says that the body is pleasured by serving. As it hears and acknowledges these words, a shudder runs through the bound limbs and across the naked skin… A warmth rises from deep inside as it surrenders and obeys.

The Voice tells the body that it will change and adapt – that it will be shaped and transformed to whatever the Voice desires… As the warmth continues to spread throughout the body, it feels itself dissolve and change. Flesh and bone melt and transmute – just as the Voice commands…

The body is gripped by a rising feeling of euphoria – it is lifted on chains of obedience and hangs weightless, suspended in space. Then the Voice releases its grip and it feels itself slowly descending into a dark, blood-warm sea.

Liquid rubber surrounds it, bathes it in an amniotic warmth of transformation. The heat spreads across the body's skin, the outer edges of sensation – then slowly seeps inwards – in through each pore. Liquid and skin becoming one.

The Voice tells the body that it is mutating: becoming a creature of pure rubber. Skin, bones, flesh: all changing – becoming flexible, pliant. Brain, senses, thought – all dissolving in the rising black tide of rubber that absorbs and transforms the body completely – and according to the Voice's command.

The body floats, cocooned – foetal-curled in the silence of its rubber womb – until the Voice comes again, commands its limbs to move, and it rises upwards, stepping from the tank made new.

Its flesh is grey and wet at first, and then turns glossy as it dries: slowly changing from flesh to black rubber... As the new skin cures, it tightens – firming and holding the body in a rubber embrace from which it can never escape...

Shudders and shivers run through the body as the transformation is completed.

Dimly, awareness spreads in response to the Voice's command: the body is aware that it stands upright, arms held straight out to allow the slow rubber mutation to take effect – layer upon layer, rubber upon rubber.

The Voice reminds the body that it is unable to move without its express command, and so the body stands perfectly still: a pillar of slowly drying rubber. It is restrained more completely by the Voice's Will than any bonds could ever effect...

Time passes, the body stands, a glossy statue. It is unaware of anything but the Voice and the pleasure spreading throughout its limbs – spreading from the tightening, rubberised skin that enfolds and restricts it.

The rubber skin that slowly becomes its own.

Finally, the Voice tells the body that now it may see.

Slowly light seeps in through its eyes and shapes begin to form within the darkness inside its head.

An image appears: a creature stands within a darkened room. Spotlights pick out its form against the darkness; they shine and glint off the thick smooth black rubber of its skin.

The rubber creature stands: feet planted firmly, arms straight out at the sides – crucified in empty space. Its rubber skin is perfect, seamless – from the soles of its feet to the naked dome of its shaved head. Even the low hang of its cock and balls is perfect in their rubberised details.

The gentle rise and fall of the creature's rubbered chest is the only visible movement…

Dog

The Voice comes out of the darkness. It tells the body to move, to lower its arms.

Slowly the arms sink to the sides: the muscles moving and flexing beneath the sheen of rubber – defined and purified by their new, glossy black skin…

Another command:

"Turn slowly around. Display yourself…"

The creature moves, and is met by multiple images of itself – reflected and repeated by the mirrors that line the walls of this darkened space… The body is smooth skinned and tightly muscled – neither hair nor blemish mars the gleaming black surface. It appears to be a statue of athletic perfection, sculpted from pure solid rubber. The only human imperfection is the dark brown eyes that stare from the naked and rubbered face – but they show no sense of recognition or awareness beyond the command of the Voice…

The Voice seems pleased with its work. It utters a phrase:

"Good boy. Your Master is pleased with your transformation"

With the words, a shudder of pure pleasure runs through the creature – visible as it wells up from deep within its body and ripples across its skin – a shudder of pleasure more intense than any orgasm: pure physical bliss at pleasing the Voice of its Master.

The Voice commands again:

"Creature – become a dog"

The creature's rubber-skinned reflected form seems to ripple before its eyes: its legs seem to buckle and fold as it sinks to the floor…

Legs shorten and fold, tuck under the body. The thighs thickening to form haunches…

A bud forms between its rounded butt cheeks. It presses outwards, then grows and extends into a thick tail: shining and glossy like the rest of its rubbered-skin…

Hands curl and fold in upon themselves. They become paws, complete with claws and pads…

The creature's back flattens and lengthens.

Its neck shrinks in upon itself and thickens as it draws the creature's head back upon the shoulders… Its throat tightens and changes. It loses the ability of speech, and becomes capable of only growls, barks and whines…

The face flattens, and the jaw lengthens – becomes a muzzle and jowls. The skull and forehead lower as its ears grow rigid and pointed.

Brown eyes glaze over as the iris spreads and becomes dark…

Between its hind legs, the cock slowly pulls in upon itself – presses up against the rubbered underbelly as a line of rubber reaches down to form a sheath. Its balls swell to hang low and exposed below its puckered black hole…

Within the body, the creature's mind also transforms and mutates: slowly dulling, knowing only loyalty, love and obedience for its Master. Knowing only the need to be owned, loved, and trained…

Slowly the whole creature transforms and changes before its eyes. It responds to the Voice's command – and ripples of pleasure shoot through its limbs with every change: the joy of transformation, and the bliss of obeying the Voice's command…

Then, with one last shudder, the transformation is complete.

A perfect rubber-dog now sits where before there had been a rubber-skinned humanoid shape. The bright lights reflect from its glossy black flanks, the dome of its head – and from the thick tail that slowly sweeps across the floor, wagging in pleasure at obeying the Voice and its Master. The dog sits – waiting, hoping, for the words that will let it know it has truly pleased…

"GOOD BOY!"

Shudders of pleasure course through the changed form. The tongue lolls out of its canine, rubbered jaws and a whine of pleasure escapes its mutated throat… Its cock twitches and swells in pure excitement and unrolls itself from the canine sheath to press and twitch against its stomach.

For a brief moment, paws that once were hands move as if to touch it – then stop, useless…

The dog whines and cocks its head to the direction of the Voice. Its rubber ears swivel – listening with new intensity for the sound of its Master's approach. Its nose twitches: catches the musk of muscles and maleness overlain with rubber.

A bark escapes its jaws with the recognition of its Master's rich scent…

The Master steps from out of the darkness.

Tall, and broad, His muscular frame glints under the lights, His muscles rippling beneath their own skin of rubber.

Smooth boots encase His feet and rise up His legs, framing them in their shining embrace. The thick cleated soles silent against the rubber-coated floor.

Tight rubber jeans tuck into the boot tops, form themselves tightly around his calves, knees and broad thighs. The rubber rises to the mound of his crotch, held firm beneath several layers and the twin zips of the sailor fronted jeans…

His broad chest is framed by a rubber biker's jacket, buckled tight around his narrow waist. Even through the thickness of the rubber, the dog can see the ripple and stretch of His muscles, the mound of his shoulders and biceps. The jacket parts slightly at the top to reveal a tight, military style shirt, stretched taught and shining over muscular pecs. The long neck of a hood is tucked into the shirt, held tightly closed by the collar and tie…

Black rubber coats even His face. Only His eyes pierce the black smoothness. They glint in the darkness as the Master approaches His creature – His newly transformed dog.

Thick gloves enfold His hands, and in their grasp hang a collar and leash…

From its rightful position on the floor, the Master appears to tower over the dog – the top of His boots level with its questing, rubbered nose and filling the creature with the heady smell of rubber and its Master…

The dog looks up into its Master's face and knows the pure pleasure of being owned and possessed. It knows that it is no longer a stray; no longer lost and confused, but owned and made new according to the Master's wishes…

The Master reaches down, pats the dog upon its domed and canine skull. In response, the dog presses its head up into the Master's hand: nuzzles and licks His rubber-clad fingers. Pure pleasure flows through its body and mind at being able to show its love for the Master who has possessed and transformed it…

Within its newly canine skull, the dog knows only the need to please and serve HIM – no memory, no thought besides these needs remains.

Newly transformed, newly enslaved, the dog is only aware of the intense pleasure it feels as its Master reaches down with His gloved hands and buckles on the collar around its neck…

It shudders as an intense wave of excitement courses through its body, and He chuckles and says:

"Come on boy: time for a walk to the club – I'm going to really enjoy showing off my new pet"

As the Master and His dog pass the many mirrors in the room, the spotlights glint off their rubber-skins. The bright light defines and reflects the two figures: one tall, rubber-skinned and with an air of complete Mastery – the other a man in a dog hood who pads across the floor on all fours.

A Master and a rubber-skinned man-dog who walks to heel on the leash that falls from the Master's gloved hands: a creature who seems to move and think so much like a real dog, tail wagging in pleasure and looking up at its Master with love and obedience…

The lights also glint off the tag that hangs from the dog's collar and the words engraved there:

"*Property of Vulcanise*"

*"…In all of them, he is my own fantasies made
flesh: the Man whom the boy within me longs to
worship – and the Man I imagine becoming…"*

Obsession

"GIVE YOURSELF UP TO THAT WHICH PLEASES, PUP…"

Even after all this time, as I read these words it is *his* voice I hear in my head: soft, firm, calm, and subtly enticing. A strong voice, a voice like a firm hand wrapped in silk – or enfolded in a silk rubber glove…

I do not really understand it, but his was a voice that spoke for my desires – spoke *to* my desires. It was as if the rubber had found a voice and spoke through him: silky smooth, quietly but irresistibly insistent. Through him, it wormed its way deep into me, into my dark recesses – calling to me like some chemically inspired siren song.

Hearing that voice I felt myself dissolve, my resolve weaken…

His voice reads the words of his e-mail back to me – and the image of him in the attachment below it captures me in the steady gaze of his eyes, shining through the glossy smoothness of his rubber hood. The gloved hand that reaches towards the camera is both beckoning and possessive – inviting me to the promise of its safe embrace, and threatening a grip from which I may never escape…

I am caught between two opposing emotions – of fear and longing. I can feel the hunger and excitement build within me – even as I feel myself falling into those eyes, listening to the soft insistence of the voice. I feel myself start to reach out for that hand through the screen…

> *"…You're a nice pup – a treasure. If you*
> *ever need a rock, I will be here…"*

A rock: steady and solid, something to cling to amidst the turmoil of my eroticized state.

But also a stone, a weight, an anchor…

It has been over a year, yet I barely know this man. I know only his image in photographs. In them his is the carefully crafted image of the perfect Leather-man: primally masculine within his leather carapace of jacket and boots – or of the Rubber Master: his body distorted and eroticized by the rubber flesh that transforms it. His eyes glint hypnotically within them all: bright and burning from within the hoods, gas masks and helmets that he wears – or they hide themselves behind mirrored glasses that reflect my own desire back to me…

In the reality of these photographs is the fantasy of a life dedicated to fetish and pleasure. In all of them, he is my own fantasies made flesh: the Man whom the boy within me longs to worship – and the Man I imagine becoming…

Perhaps it is because I was suggestible at the times we have spoken – already drifting in a trance-like state from hours of browsing fetish images on the 'net and swapping fantasies with long-term rubber-buddies on IRC... When his nic would buzz up on the screen, I would already be swimming in a highly charged state of erotic tension brought on by autosuggestion and frustrated desire. In this state, his air of relaxed command could so easily become the soothing and commanding voice of the hypnotist: encouraging my already entranced brain to yield and accept his suggestions – suggestions already so close to the images it was itself generating...

––––––––

From the first time we spoke, it was as if he had reached into my head and pulled out my deepest fantasies. With guiltless ease, he spoke of the darkest images that swirl around my poppers-soaked brain in moments of weakness. Spoke of them as his own – spoke and made them real.

His words conjured thoughts of rubber-flesh and transformation. Of people remade in the image of their fetish. Of bodies shaved and rubberised into unrecognisable anonymity. Of minds guided to embrace a new rubber identity by total immersion in pleasure and fantasy... His words spoke too of half-human hybrids given over to pleasure and service. Of men transformed into dogs, and alien-implants that altered their hosts into rubberised creatures... Of men whose bodies and minds had been altered and transformed by the intensity of pleasure to which they have sacrificed themselves – and by the hands and minds of those who safely guide them to that perfect surrender...

Of lives changed, and bodies given over to the service of these masterful, transforming men...

Perhaps it was a conscious act on his part: to lead, suggest, and pervert. More likely, it was merely an act of transference by my sex-confused brain. Maybe it was even fate! But, whether by accident or by design, that connection was made all the same – and each time we spoke the connection was strengthened… Each time I heard or read his words I felt myself associate him more and more with my rubber fantasies – and my increasingly intense rubber desires…

Slowly, I felt his words become the governing voice of the rubber within me: the guide and mentor to my building urge for rubber surrender – and felt myself willingly embrace and accept his command and control over me…

The more his soft, commanding voice spoke of his dark fantasies of rubber and transformation, the more they became my fantasies too – and the stronger my hunger and need for them became.

I found myself caught in vivid dreams of myself transformed – myself surrendered to a hunger that built into an ecstasy which overwhelmed my mind and transformed my body…

I found myself straining to hear his quiet voice as I felt it guide and beckon me onwards – deeper into the fantasy, deeper into the hunger and the desire…

Felt the rubber within me develop a personality of its own – bonded to his voice and invoked by his coded call…

And still his talks with me delved deeper, reached further into fantasy and perversity. His voice always guiding, encouraging, advising – and subtly Mastering…

———

*"Remember pup: as I build my life, so I
am - as I am, so I build my life!"*

Gradually I found myself collecting more and more rubber gear – buying gloves and gas masks, suits and sleep sacks, piss-funnels and re-breather hoods. Each purchase following one of our talks and directly inspired by the fantasies we had discussed.

Each item was carefully unwrapped from its delivery package, radiating with the promise of further surrender and absorption to the rubber within me. But each was then carefully stored away until I could be alone and free to call him – so that *his* would be the voice that ordered me to put on each item and to feel the slave within me arise at its touch… His voice the trigger that made each piece of rubber come to life in my hands.

It was always his voice, accompanying each new item, each new experience: his voice, guiding me, restraining me, tantalising me with the deferred fulfilment of my hunger…

His voice that finally taught me to love and worship the rubber – and to surrender myself to it fully.

I remember one conversation in particular – over my first set of thick rubber gloves.

He had me hold them first: to look at them and see how reflections flowed across the smooth glossy surface, how every subtle movement made the blackness ripple and flash with light. He then had me press them to my face and to breathe deeply – crooned encouragement as I inhaled their sweet and chemical smell deep into me. His soft voice told me to let the smell call to the rubber within me…

Only when he could hear my soft moans and knew that I was falling under their spell did he allow me to draw them slowly onto my hands: telling me to feel their tight but yielding touch enfold me – to feel the combined loss of sensation and the increased sexual charge as my hands were encased within their thickened rubber skin…

He had me study these newly transformed hands – compare them with his own gloved hands in the pictures he sent me. He told me to see the way the rubber masked and altered my body into a reflection of his own...

He then had me stand before a mirror and explore my face and body – to allow myself to realise that these gloved hands were but extensions of his own rubbered body. Telling me to feel my own rubber-touch as coming from outside of myself – to come to feel that the muted sensation within the gloves was because those gloved hands were no longer mine at all, but his. To see how the rubber possessed me and transformed my own hands into *HIS*...

And then – when he could hear my grunted surrender to his suggestion – only then did he finally let me smell and taste those rubbered hands. He had me draw those industrial fingers across my face, stroke my lips, feel them as they cupped my nose – breathe deeply and let myself sink into the smell and the touch...

And then his voice was telling me how much I wanted to lick his gloved hands: my tongue obediently licking each finger, lovingly – bathing it in my own spit – tasting their peppery sweetness. Had me feel the sensual slide of their lubricated surface over my lips, tongue and teeth...

Entranced and aroused, my hunger built under his suggestion and encouragement – and I found myself moaning and sighing as first one, then another, and then another of those gloved fingers slid into my hot and hungry mouth. I could *feel* how each gloved and shining finger was *his* finger, and I sucked and licked at them hungrily, greedily. I allowed myself to become lost in these sensations as I felt myself fed by him and by my new rubber skin – felt myself opening to him and to the rubber. Felt myself hungering for his skin, his words, and his guidance. And finally felt myself yielding: surrendering to his voice, his hands and my own desire...

Lost in rubber and trance I accepted everything that he said to me. I found myself listening, ears cocked, to hear his encouraging voice as he told me what a good boy I was, how proud he was of his rubber boy. Telling me how the moans and growls that escaped me pleased him – how my little whines and barking moans let him know how much his little *rubber pup* was embracing his hunger and need – and how the sound of my panting breathing showed him that his rubber pup was coming close to his full rubber transformation…

And under his subtly worded suggestion I found myself flooded with a new set of images and feelings: began to feel and see myself as a dog – *His* dog – His pup and His pet…

I found myself recognising and embracing these feelings of animal simplicity, obedience, and loyalty: found myself listening to his voice as he encouraged his rubber pup to express himself like the dog he was – and I found my throat opening as deep barks escaped from my lengthening jaw, as the animal within me found its voice.

I found my gloved hands curling up upon themselves and becoming paws. I felt my body thrill and my mind dull as the pup I was becoming felt the pride of his Master – and I heard that pride reflected in his voice as he told me what a good pup I was. I listened intently to how my Master would treat his pup, care for him, help him to fully embrace the transformation he now hungered for – and felt waves of excitement build as my Master told me how his pup could feel his Master's gloved hand stroke and pet his little rubber pup…

Slowly, I felt this new identity solidify and the old "me" melt away. I felt my body responding as my Master's voice encouraged his pup to hump his gloved hand like a true rubber doggy would… I found my hips grinding as I instinctively humped his surrogate fist – until my dog-cock spewed its doggy-cum into the slick warmth of the rubber. And then I found my rubbered tail wagging as I hungrily lapped the salty-sweet treat from my Master's fingers – barking my excitement and love in acceptance of this new k9 reality and rubber identity…

And it *was* a new identity: a reality which I embraced fully and excitedly. A reality that I wanted and lusted for – a new animal identity

I had fantasised over in the past – and one that this Voice was now helping to make real…

————

Every new rubber item was like this: his voice guiding me to a full appreciation of its impact upon me. Each new piece used as a tool to bring me further in and deeper down into acceptance of my own desires and his guiding voice: sometimes as dog, sometimes as slave – but always and only in rubber…

With him as my rubber-guide and mentor, I found myself surrendering to myself and the rubber within me in a way I have never before felt – a surrender beyond all the adolescent angst and fear of teenage bedroom wanks…

In trance, the need to serve and obey him grew overwhelming… I felt like a child again, and eagerly embraced both that hunger and dependence: the need to please and make my Master proud…

The more I embraced my surrender to him, the more I needed that surrender and his control. Under his increasing dominance, I felt myself become weak and pliable for him. I found myself *wanting* him to tell me what to feel, what to think: to tell me how and what to *be*.

And it felt so *good.* So good to relax and surrender to his Voice – to the control and the pleasure I felt in opening up for him. And each and every time that surrender washed deeper – and the pleasure of obedience affected me stronger…

With his voice as my guide, I found myself becoming the rubber that had always fascinated me so deeply. I found myself becoming both slave and dog: embracing the rubber that had previously been a symbol of my own sad perversity and degradation, but was now badge of a new and simplified form of life and desire – a new life born of surrender and transformation.

Eventually, I even found myself beginning to sleep curled on my side and dreaming as a dog. I began to think of myself only as rubbered, as canine, and owned. I found myself confused and uncomfortable when I saw my 'raw' and nakedly pink skin – found myself arranging to be alone, so that I could gratefully pull on my 'true' black rubber skin and doggy mask, buckling on my dog collar and living on all fours…

In time, I even found myself contentedly licking my 'paws' clean after meals unquestioningly eaten from a bowl on the floor… I found myself only able to find release on all fours and humping my Master's surrogate rubbered hand, with my Master's voice in my puppy-head, growling his encouragement and pushing me further down, further in to my complete acceptance of this newly canine rubber identity…

There was a beauty and dark simplicity as his voice suggested and prompted ever deeper – and my body and mind responded to him, and hungered for him. An obsession in the way I hungered for how my desire, his voice, and the rubber conspired to alter and change me into his image and his desire…

And finally, a desperation in how I hungered for that final and complete surrender: an urgency that drew me to beg him to let me fully and finally give myself to him – and to surrender to the irrevocable transformation of everything that was once me into becoming his beautifully Mastered and anonymous rubber-thing…

It was then – only once he heard my desperate pleading, and knew that I had surrendered completely to my hunger and obsession – only *then* that he finally gave me the orders that he had guided me towards across all those endless months. Finally gave me permission to meet him in person.

It was then – when he heard my desperate pleading: knew that I was irrevocably lost and surrendered completely to the hunger and obsession that he had created – only then did he command me to come to him: ready to surrender everything in order to become the property and pet of the real man behind the voice – the true Master of the rubber-desires that he had kindled within me.

To hear his voice and to finally and completely give myself up to that which pleases…

"…a young, nervous lad – beads of sweat glossing his newly shaved head – stands at a normal-looking door in a northern English town…"

A northern kennel

A young, nervous lad – beads of sweat glossing his newly shaved head – stands at a normal-looking door in a northern English town.

He anxiously glances both ways down the street, and then looks down at his feet, encased in tall glossy black Rangers. Every line of his body reveals the internal fight against fear and nervous anxiety – the debate whether to run or stay.

He swallows nervously, licks his lips from a dry mouth, rubs a damp palm down the side of his jeans…. but then that nervously rubbing hand drifts up to the tight denim across his crotch, cups the hard curve of arousal that betrays his real excitement…

For a moment, the hand stays cupped, and his nervous face shifts into a decision. A small nod to himself – a brief squaring of shoulders – then he reaches out and pushes the bell.

Nothing for a few moments, and then the door opens. A dark figure stands in the gloomy interior. The weak sunlight glints from his leather jeans and heavy Wesco boots. No words are spoken, but the boy ducks his head slightly, looks down at those shining boots in nervous respect… The figure watches for a moment, then gives the smallest of gestures: shifting slightly to one side. The boy takes his cue – steps to the door and over the threshold.

Briefly, they brush against each other in the closeness of the doorway. The boy hesitates, and finally looks up into the figure's eyes.

"So, pup – you really ready for this…?"

The boy swallows again – licks his lips – looks deep into the man's eyes:

"Yes Sir – please Sir. Please: I want to be your dog!"

With a smile, the figure reaches one hand up to cup the back of the boy's head – with the other he slowly pushes the door closed.

It clicks shut with the sound of finality…

————

Inside.

Underground.

The basement of the house…

It is a cool, clean, empty space – with blank walls and a black and white tiled floor.

This is a quiet space – hidden away beneath the house, beneath the street. A perfect place in which to escape the world and all its fears and disappointments…

In a corner stands a large welded metal cage. Its floor is a wipe-able rubber mat, and a large padlock holds the front door closed. It is a locked space, a safe space – a place to be kept in, a place to be safe in.

In the centre of the room the boy now stands: booted feet planted solidly, hands behind his back and his shoulders squared, his head bowed. He stands and waits in respectful silence.

In the corner – silent and comfortable in a leather chair – sits the man from the doorstep. His one booted foot rests on the other. The shadows seem to cling to Him as He sits and watches the boy: obedient, patient, waiting for His commands…

He lets the boy wait a few moments more, then He gets up, walks over – enjoys seeing the young man tense a little.

The Man walks around him slowly – inspecting the boy with His eyes. The boy trembles slightly under His silent gaze…

Finally He speaks:

"So, you want to be a dog, boy?"

He enjoys seeing the trembling increase – the nervous flick of a tongue; enjoys seeing the boy fight with his urge to look up from the floor – meet this Man's eyes… Instead, a shaky voice answers:

"Yes Sir – please SIR – I want to be your dog, SIR"

"Ah, but boy: to be a dog – to be my dog – there will have to be some changes!"

The Man reaches out to the trembling lad – places a hand upon the back of his head. He gently strokes the naked scalp, and smiles as He feels the tension relax a little as the lad gives an involuntary sigh.

"Do you think you can make those changes boy? Do you think you have what it takes to be my dog?"

"SIR, yes SIR! Please SIR!"

The boy almost shouts his response – and the Man smiles once again to see the urgency of this young man's hunger.

"To become my pup you will need to be stripped and shaved – then your body encased in a glossy rubber coat. You will have your hands turned into paws, and your head transformed by a hood. You will be made to look as close to the real dog that you are – maybe even with a tail… Do you think that you could cope with that boy? Do you think you could cope with being made into a real rubber-dog…?"

Once more He is pleased to see the boy shudder – and notes the hard curve of his arousal in his jeans. He smiles at how the boy seems to have lost his voice and can merely nod his head. And then He hears, so quietly, the lad's voice – choked, urgent and trembling:

"Yes Sir, I know Sir. Please SIR!"

The Man strokes down onto the boy's neck, rubs an ear:

"My pup will need to be trained in whatever manner I see fit. It might be drugged or hypnotised, brainwashed and reprogrammed: whatever I deem necessary to help it become a true pup. Can you surrender to that boy? Will you devote yourself to becoming a real dog? My dog?"

The stroking hand stops, cups the boy's chin and tilts the face up – studies the slight tremble in the lip and the wet, downcast eyes…

"Can you embrace your own fantasies, pup, and live like a dog – as MY dog?"

Almost whispering now, the boy finally looks up into His eyes – and the Man reads there all the hunger and need and surrender that He needed to see:

"Yes SIR, please SIR. Let me be your dog SIR!"

"OK pup, then let's begin…"

———————

It is months later.

Outside – beyond the cool white walls of the basement – the world moves on, unaware and uncaring.

In the corner of the basement room, inside the padlocked cage, curled up on a warm woollen blanket: a figure all in black. The low lighting reflects off its glossy polished skin as the figure breathes, gentle and slow.

Here in the dark, in the warmth, the figure sleeps.

In the silence, the soft drone of a recorded hypnotic voice can be heard: an endlessly loop that mutters barely audible suggestions and assurances – and quietly reprograms its silent listener in its sleep…

In the house up above: the sound of boots as they walk across a wooden floor, and then the click as a key turns in the door.

The figure in the cage hears the sound. It stirs in its sleep: a small wordless whine escapes it, and it slowly raises its head and turns towards the sound. The dim lights move across the shining skin and glint along a long muzzle and sharp pointed ears.

Boots creak on the wooden stairs. In an instant the dog in the cage is up on all fours, ears pricked, muzzle raised and sniffing the air expectantly. It almost seems to dance on its paws in excitement as the boots finally step down from the stairs and onto the tiled floor.

The dog presses its muzzle against the cage door. It stares through the bars as its Master moves across the floor – hungrily takes in His boots and leather…

"*Hello pup!*"

The Man reaches in through the bars, and rubs a glossy ear. With a happy yelp of pleasure, the pup leans into His hand. A pink tongue lolls from the muzzle as it gives a long growling whine: a wordless expression of pleasure and devotion…

"*How did my pup sleep then, eh? – I hope the basement wasn't too cold for you!*"

He gives the pup one last scratch, and then moves away from the cage. He clicks a button on the small stereo: the quietly hypnotic recorded voice fades into silence…

"*I think that should be enough of that tape for tonight – I don't want to completely scramble my pup's brains. At least, not yet…*"

He moves towards shelves on the wall and starts getting down bowls and packets of food. All the time He talks to the pup in the cage. The pup watches, head cocked: eagerly drinking in every word and every movement.

The Master turns. He sets down a cold metal bowl on the floor and cool water slops over the side. He reaches into a pocket and removes a small pillbox – He takes out a small blue pill and drops it into the water. He removes a small bottle from another pocket, and carefully adds a few drops of its contents to the bowl as well.

Satisfied, He stands, moves towards the cage and unlocks the padlock. Inside the pup sits taller, a small bark escapes its glossy muzzle.

"*Good pup! It must be hot in that suit – your Man thinks it must be time for a little drink…*"

The pup looks towards the bowl. Drool drips from its tongue in thirst, but it does not move a muscle or run for the water that it so obviously craves.

"*GOOD PUP! – you're learning!*"

The Master waits one more moment. The pup's muscles tense in eager anticipation, but it waits for the command…

"*OK pup – DRINK!*"

With the words, the pup lunges forward out of the cage. Paws skitter on the tiles in its eager rush. It catches itself from falling, and then it plunges its head down into the bowl. Its tongue is long and pink as it laps up the cool clear water – and the chemical additives that it now contains…

As it drinks, its smooth rubberised arse is raised high, moving back and forth: wagging an invisible tail…

With a laugh, the Master strokes a hand down the glossy rubberised back. From the bowl, the pup lets out a contented "WUFF!" – but it does not stop its eager drinking… The Master watches proudly.

"*Good dog! Drink it all up now!*"

The pup raises its head – the rubber muzzle glossy, wet, and dripping.

It looks up at its Master and gives a deep happy bark – so deep that its chest and belly contract in the rubber as it pushes each bark from deep down inside of itself – expressing itself in the only way it seems to know how.

The physical effort of each primal bark seems to arouse the dog, and the glossy sheathed cock jumps and thumps against its rubberised belly.

"GOOD DOG!!!"

The Master laughs, and rubs the pup's head – strokes down its back and pats its rubberised arse. His other hand rests on His own crotch – equally as aroused by this creatures' show of animal affection and pleasure…

From a pocket, the Master pulls a rag and another bottle. He tips a little of the contents into the cloth, then holds it to the dog's nose as if to wipe the water from its muzzle. The pup's head buzzes and its heart beats harder as it breathes in the sweet, masculine, chemical scent – and a hungry "WUUFFF!" bubbles up from deep within it…

The Master reaches down and cups the dog's head as the medications start to take effect. As though desperate for support, the pup leans its body into His legs. Its head seems to grow heavy and sinks into His hands. It tries to look up through the hood – up into the Master's face. Another, quieter, questioning bark escapes it…

"It's OK pup – let it go," He croons at his suddenly groggy dog. *"Poor little pup! It's OK – good dog – let go to your Man now…"*

All the time, He strokes and pets the rubber skin – strokes the head, scratches the ears…

He kneels down onto one knee, carefully moves His feet and legs to provide more support for the dog's weight as it takes another deep inhalation from the scented rag. Its entire body now leans into His legs: submissively, completely, trustingly…

With His touch, a shudder travels over the dog's rubber skin and underlying muscle. A "WUFF!" escapes through the muffling rag; bleary eyes struggle to focus up onto His face.

"Yes pup – your Man sees you! That's a good dog! Let go pup – let go to the feelings. Let go to the pup you know you are"

Holding and stroking the dog's head, the Master stares deep into the spreading blackness of its eyes – croons support and encouragement to His pup. Looking for the surrender and acceptance that lets Him know this dog is ready…

"Y*eah – my good little pup – my drugged and fucked-up little pet… Let go pup: let go to the changes… Let your Man help you – let Him transform you. Let him make you the rubber-dog that you know you are – and begged Him to make you…!*"

With each word, the dog's cock starts to pulse and swell between its rubberised haunches – the tapering red head pushing further from the sheath that holds it to its belly.

"*Good dog!*" the Boss encourages and croons – "*Yeah – that's my horny little pup!*"

He licks a finger, reaches down, and circles it around the throbbing head…

Unnaturally bright eyes blink and stare from the rubberised muzzle – gaze up into its Master's eyes.

Another bark bubbles up from inside the rubberised form… with it the dog seems to shake itself and it pulls itself up onto all fours: the head raised high and the back curved – like a dog on show – tail high and proud…

"*GOOD BOY!!*"

The Master strokes and pats His pet: the circling finger pushing into the sheath as the pup's cock drools precum… His other hand wraps around its hanging balls and gives them a gentle tug…

The dog gives a deep "WUFF!" of appreciation and wags its arse harder. The Master smiles to see the tension in its haunches as it tries not to hump itself into His warm strong hand.

"Yeah – good dog! That's it, ain't it pup? – you're a horny little pup – MY pervert dog!"

"WUUFFF!"

The dog leans its head over into the Master's side. A pink tongue pokes out of the rubber hood and licks His hand – His wrist – His arm… The carefully administered stimulants working with the rubber and the Master's words to shift the pup's awareness, its perception of reality: every word, every stroke taking it deeper into the dog it resembles and is now becoming.

"GOOD BOY! – yeah: that's my pup!"

The Master looks over His dog: takes in its glossy rubber skin, the mitted paws and hooded head with pride and possession.

He releases its cock and pats the wagging arse…

With His touch, the pup wags even harder. It looks up into His eyes and gives a questioning bark…

"Ah! – my pup is missing something is it?"

The dog goes down onto its mitted front paws – raises its arse in the air and gives a deep playful "ARRUUUFF!"

"OK then pup – 1 second…"

He moves over to the cupboards. The pup makes to move with him, but the Master turns:

"NO pup! – Sit! STAY!"

The dog's rubberised rump instantly hits the floor – and its cock jumps at this show of its own unquestioning obedience.

"GOOD BOY!" – and the cock bounces even higher at His praise…

The Master turns from the cupboards, a large piece of moulded rubber in his hands…

"The last piece of the puzzle…"

He smiles to see his pup, sitting obedient and alert. Then:

"HEEL BOY!"

The pup is a blur as it skitters across the floor: eager to obey and please its Master. Its rubberised body wraps around His legs until it sits tight against His left side, head looking up and leaning into His hip.

"GOOD BOY!"

He lets the pup scent the rubber on His hands for a moment, then:

"On my Boots, Pup!"

At the command, the pup whips around to sit in front of its Master. With its tailless arse raised high in the air, it buries its head down onto His boots and takes a long shuddering sniff of the well-oiled leather. With another deep and appreciative "ARRUUFF!" the pup greedily starts to work on its Master's beautiful boots: the pink tongue shoots out and licks from toe to heel – slicking the leather in wet drool. With each lick, it seems to lose itself more completely into the smell and taste of its Master.

With His pup busily showing its devotion to His boots, the Master reaches out and strokes the rubber of its arse.

"Such a nice arse – but it's just not a dog's arse, is it pup? You can't have a pup without a tail to wag, eh…?"

Muzzle buried deep into its Master's boot leather, the pup can only let out a muffled "WUFF" of agreement…

"That's it pup – you lose yourself in your Man's leather whilst He attends to things."

He reaches into a pocket, pulls out a clear rubber glove – pulls it onto His hand. With the other He reaches down and probes the smooth rubber covering the dog's glossy crack…

"Ah – here it is…!"

Lubed rubber fingers slip through a reinforced hole in the rubber – and into His dog. With a muffled grunt and bark, the dog goes still. It pants and drools into the warm wet leather as it struggles to open itself to the probing lubing fingers that slowly, gently, expertly fuck its arse…

"Good boy – you just relax and eat boots pup – open up your puppy fuck-hole for your Man…"

One circling finger still inside His pup, He picks up the rubber tail plug. Lube shines off the large rubber bulb at its base as He brings it around to His pups now twitching hungry arse.

Buried in its worship of His boot leather, the hooded head is groaning and grunting – taking deep sniffs of its Man's leather. With each panted breath it seems to relax more, almost as if His smell brings it deeper into submission and acceptance…

Lubed and glistening, the large plug is pressed up against the tight ring of muscle in the dog's arse. Hungry from the Master's attentions, the muscles twitch within the hole in the smooth rubberised suit…

"OK pup – here you go: here's your tail…!"

With a firm slow push, the Master squeezes the plug into the yielding ring of muscle… As its hole stretches open, the dog pants harder and works its face deeper into its Master's boot leather – hungrily drinking in His smell and warmth and touch – drawing strength from Him to take this pain, to accept it and let it change it for Him…

With a final push, the plug slips in all the way. The tight hole squeezes shut around the tapered base…

With its muzzle buried deep in its Man's boots, wet with drool and polish, the dog gives a muffled grunt of confusion and satisfaction. It raises its head, looks over one shoulder – and a startled bark escapes it at the sight of the foot-long tapering rubber tail that now extends from its smooth glossy arse…!

The rubber tail flexes and moves with the pup's startled movement – and another, deeper grunt is forced from its throat as the vibration travels down the rubber and into the plug buried deep and filling its hole.

It twitches its inner muscles again: testing, exploring. With each twitch, the plug rubs against the swell of its prostate, whilst the whole length of the outer rubber taper moves and wags just like a real dog's tail…

Watching, the Master smiles:

"Yeah pup – that's it – wag your tail like a real puppy!"

With his words the dog gives a big WUUFF!!! – and gives a shake of its arse that sets the tail thrashing. As each vibration travels down the rubber and into the plug, the movement drives the dog even wilder – and its cock bobs and pulses in time.

"OK pup – NOW you are starting to look like my dog!"

With His words, the dog barks loudly – tail wagging hard and sheathed cock bouncing and dripping onto the tiled floor.

"Does the pup want to see itself? Does my pup want to see how it really is its Master's little rubber dog…?"

The Master snaps a lead onto the collar around His dog's neck. He leads the pup to the wall where a floor length mirror fills the view.

As the pup sees its own reflection it tenses for a moment in confusion – almost as if it does not recognise the dog it sees there. It holds back and pulls on the chain. A momentary look of fear flashes through its eyes and its hackles raise; a deep threatening growl rumbles up from its throat…

The Man laughs – and gives the chain a quick tug.

"Come on you daft pup! Who's this then, eh? Who's the big black rubber dog?"

The pup sniffs, and the rubber muzzle twitches and moves. Cautious eyes stare out of the glossy face. A deep questioning "WUFF…?" escapes the muzzle as the pup moves forward – almost touches noses with its own glossy reflection in the mirror…

The hooded head swings around to look up at the Master where He stands behind His dog, watching. It gives another "wuff…?"

"Yes pup – that's you! – you're a real doggy now!"

The Master crouches down onto one knee beside His dog – drapes an arm around the pup's back and meets its questioning eyes in the mirror.

"Go on pup – look. Look deep.

*"See the truth: you **are** a dog – just like I said you would be.*

"Look: you have a nice glossy rubber coat – a beautiful muzzle, perky ears – a real doggy's face… Yes, pup – look deeply at yourself now, and see your true face at last…"

The Master continues to stare into His pup's eyes and gently strokes its rubber head and back. His hands and eyes confirm each word, each Truth…

The pup watches its own reflection – and stares deep into its Master's eyes – accepting, confirming, and surrendering to the Truth in His words with each touch…

*"See pup: you **are** a dog. You have a muzzle, you have paws… you now even have a tail…!"*

The thick rubber tapered tail thumps upon the floor in response, and the pup leans its glossy body into the Master's leg. Beneath the rubber, the eyes shine as the pup feeds on its own reflection – drinking in this new reality…

The Master notices and deepens His voice at His dog's entrancement. He croons the Truths the pup needs to hear: repeats the words that have droned and whispered into its sleeping head from the recorded hypnosis tapes for many months…:

"Yes pup – look at yourself. You are a rubber-dog, aren't you pup? You're MY rubber-dog, pup.

"You must be a dog, pup: just look at yourself – look and know it's true. FEEL it, pup. See it: your rubber skin, your lovely paws, that beautiful alert doggy face – that thick glossy rubber tail… Yes pup – you are a dog.

"You look like a dog. You're on all fours just like a dog. You've got a lovely big black tail like a proper dog. Fuck, pup, you've even got my collar on, just like a pet dog would wear…

See, I told you pup: you are a dog – just a beautiful rubber pet for your Master!"

With each word, the pup's eyes shine more. Its sheathed cock throbs and its tail beats a slow rhythm against the floor. Its rubberised and transformed body leans harder into the Master's leg in surrender as the rubber, and the plug, and the drugs, and the hypnotic reprogramming, and the moment itself all conspire to slip it away from reality and into its fantasy… conspiring to erode the boy's mind ever deeper. Eating away at his concept of himself. Feeding into his perversion and desires – reaching into his fantasy and making it real. Making *him* real: a real dog, here and now. A dog for his Master. A dog for his Man.

His humanity surrendered for a rubber skin and a collar – and the knowledge that it will be cared for, and free to love without question…

"*Yes pup – my pup – my beautiful rubber doggie*"

The Boss strokes and fusses His pet – rubs over its smooth and glossy rubber skin. His hands rub and probe and press and stroke. Under the touch and the words and the need the dog shudders with pleasure and hunger.

A small whine escapes from its jaws. It leans its head over to its Master, gently licks His face, His nose, His neck…

"*Yeah! – good pup!*"

The Master laughs – grabs His dog's jowls and kisses the end of its nose.

The dog gives a big bark of love and devotion. The eyes within its hood now show the barest glimmer of awareness or humanity.

The pup is so close now: so close to letting go forever – so close to becoming the true pup its Master wants him to be…

The Master sees it too – smiles His smile – and strokes His dog's head. He stares into His boy's puppy-dog eyes. He drinks in the surrender and obedience that He finds there – and greedily watches the slow fading of self-awareness and humanity…

"Almost there now pup" He quietly whispers…

The pup's ears perk, and it cocks its head: a purely instinctive, canine movement devoid of self-consciousness. A paw reaches up and rests on the Master's leg; the tongue pokes out – pink and wet… A small whine escapes its muzzle.

The Master strokes that doggy face once more – then He turns the pup's head to face the mirror. He watches it look at its own reflection one last time – and sees what He needed to see: sees the bleary eyes focus momentarily and the sheathed cock stiffen one last time…

With a grin, He reaches into a pocket. He pulls out a tight rubber glove, and then lubes his palm…

"One last trigger from the brainwashing file now pup. I know I've not let you cum during the months of preparation, but now it's time to make use of all that pent up need – to use it to power the last true transformation. You see pup, to be a dog – a REAL dog – you are going to need to be milked dry like stud dog would be… One last little surrender as you give me the last dregs of your humanity. One final stream of cum that will seal you forever into the rubber. One last surrender to make this all real – to make you fully mine…"

He holds the pup's gaze, locks onto it in the reflection. He knows that it can see itself now completely – that it sees the rubber, sees the hood and the paws and the tail… He knows that it sees all of the modifications that He has made to its body – but sees them now as real.

He knows that His training and programming have taken root in its mind as He sees it look at the rubberised hood and muzzle and think of itself as this: as this hood, this skin, this dog…

The lubed palm reaches down – gently strokes the stiffening dog-cock that pushes from the sheath… With a grunt and whine, the dog wags its tail, goes up onto all fours – raises its arse and gives its tail an involuntary wag.

With each lubed stroke the dog melts further into the rubber and the boy dissolves – forgets and surrenders. He surrenders himself completely to the moment: to these feelings, to this need. Surrenders to becoming what he has always wanted to be: a dog, just a dog – a rubber dog for his Master – a loved and cared for and obedient pet…

The dog helplessly humps, and starts to growl and whine as it does so. It is lost in the moment – given over now only to the animal pleasure of fucking.

The Master stares into His dog's eyes – strokes its cock with expert, lubed fingers. He watches hungrily as He sees the boy dissolve into the rubber – into being His dog… He smiles as He feels the dog respond and start to hump His hand – involuntary, instinctive – just as His programming has told it to do.

Somewhere inside, the boy knows that this will be the last time he will cum as a boy – that in this final act of surrender he will give permission to his Master's programming to completely rewire his brain and make him a dog forever. The boy knows this, and yet is powerless to stop himself. He finds himself greedily pushing his lubed and sheathed cock ever deeper, ever harder into his Master's tightly enfolding rubber gloved hand. He is betrayed by his body, lost in the pleasure – finds himself willingly giving himself as the rubber overwhelms his senses and the need to cum becomes all that he can think of – all he wants and needs.

The Master knows His dog is close. Close to letting go – close to cumming, close to surrendering. He can feel the swell of its sheathed cock, and knows that it is on the edge of shooting out the last dregs of its humanity and becoming purely His dog: permanently bonded to Him and to this new k9 identity.

He greedily watches its reflection, sees the muscles move and clench as the lights ripple over the rubber skin – watches as the dog's legs brace and its back curves: the boy instinctively taking on the natural stance of the dog. He stares into its reflected eyes – and sees the dog inside his boy growing, seeping into every cell of its body and mind.

Finally, He sees the dark swell of His boy's pupils as the inner walls of his mind give way and the dog-mind overwhelms the last shreds of his humanity and washes them away forever…

And into His palm the Master feels the first kicking pulses of His dog's new cock, as with a huge deep bark and growl His new dog finally cums – shooting thick wads of dog-spunk over His hands, His jeans, His boots. His dog mindlessly humping His hand: shoulders braced, tail thrashing, head and neck raised high.

He smiles as His pup finally cums like the dog he wished to be – finally cums *as* a dog. Cumming for the first time, cumming for the last time.

The Master smiles, and at last is able to take full possession, as His dog cums and surrenders and seals itself to its fate. And becomes *His* forever:

His dog, His pup – His pet…

"…PROUD to let the world know what I am:
My Master's dog, His perverted pup,
His devoted rubber hound…"

Give!

I am a blissfully blank and obedient pup: adrift and relaxed and listening to the hypnosis file that buzzes and croons in my headphones. I sigh as I surrender to the trance – happy and horny and humping and helpless…

This morning found me awakening from a dream of running 4-legged through a field, my muzzle raised to catch a half-remembered scent on the wind. I awoke to find myself curled on my side – my hands curled to paw-like fists and my legs drawn up to my chest like the haunches of a true dog.

Awoke to realise how often I now naturally act in instinctively dog-like ways…

Lying there, half awake, I realised that I welcome these small changes: that they make me feel ever closer to my Master, and more appreciative of all that He has done for me in helping me to find this simple and primal identity. Thinking of Him made my heart swell with devotion: wanting only to be all that I can for Him. Needing to love Him and serve Him and make Him proud of me.

I finally dragged myself from the bed. I did my morning routine of push-ups and core-work and stretching, then headed out for a run across the fields outside my home – letting myself relax into the loping rhythm as my mind replayed the dream and imagining myself to be that 4-legged pup once more. I let myself become absorbed in the pleasurable feeling of my body moving: fit and firm, strong and flexible – ready for the physical demands that being my Master's dog puts upon me, and knowing that it helps me look my best in the confining rubber that He loves so much.

As I ran, I was also driven by the knowledge that once I had completed my physical training, then it would be time to train my mind…

And so now here I sit: blissfully dehumanised and anonymous in my full rubber – my aching muscles warmed and compressed by a one-piece suit that fully encases and transforms me from man to much-loved pet.

My head is sheathed beneath two hoods: held tight, safe, and controlled. The double layer of rubber makes each breath a slight struggle – but it also fills my head with the heady scent of rubber and my own arousal. My ears are muffled within the enfolding rubber, and the headphones that pump my Master's words into my receptive mind. The hood's pin-prick eyes restrict and funnel my sight, so that I can only stare at the computer screen before me. Images of pups and Masters strobe and flicker there, echoing the subliminal verbal commands that pump in my ears – telling me to simply relax and embrace my primal dog-boy nature – to simply BE, and nothing more…

If I do look away from the screen and down at myself all I can see is the rubber… If I touch myself, all I feel is the rubber… The rubber that encases me in glossy black insulation, and distracts my mind away from my unreal 'human' identity. It comes to feel as though all I KNOW is the rubber: its tight irresistible wetness that snaps me back to the reality of my helpless subordination – its enfolding heat that dissolves me into the primal desire that pumps through the core of my boy-hood.

I am blissfully lost. Deliciously surrendered to the rubber that tightly controls my body and insulates me mind – that acts as a conduit to the desires at the perverted heart of me. The rubber that coats and confines the truly submissive hole in my mind that only my Master can fill…

I feel the tight rubber across my chest as it resists every breath – feel that tightness quiet and still any movement and pull me back to passive absorption. The gag in my mouth is the cock from which I drink of my Master's Will.

My helpless arousal twitches and leaks within a slickly lubed sheath, buried beneath layers of controlling tightness – whilst deep inside the core of my boy-sex I feel the electrified plug that fills and teases and stirs hunger only my Master can release…

I am confined, defined, converted, and perverted – my body restricted, and teased, and brought to the edge of release and surrender – then held there, aching, until the moment is right. Whilst deep within the confining, sweat-slick layers of my blissfully inhuman cocoon, my mind is helpless and blissful and blank – a fluid and receptive oil-black sea that absorbs and reflects the sharp-bright glory of Master's words, Master's Will.

The images flash and seer into these half-lidded eyes, this head is filled only with the throb and pump of the music and the repeating mantra of submission… The rubber breathes deep and relaxes before the familiar onslaught – embraces the true reality of its programmed identity and the bliss of being fully and hopelessly controlled and obedient.

Within the irresistible rubber cocoon, the hum-mind slowly surrenders and becomes purely dog-mind – it sunders and dissolves as the programming overwhelms all thought, all resistance – and releases the truly *primal* pup from within. Every barking breath, every humping twitch only confirms and deepens the blissful truth of my Master's reality and my joyful confession, panted into the confines of my rubber hood – spoken in truth and devotion:

"I am only a pup, my Master's rubber-hound"…

Confessing, surrendering – until the pulsing and flashing and the slick tight rubber embrace of my skin squeeze every drop of humanity from my mind – and all thought dissolves to my Master's remembered command of "GIVE!"

At this word of release – of PERMISSION – my tight and painful dog-balls shudder and pump the pure essence of my submission from my straining dog-knot – up past the plug and the straps and the rings that hold that moment of release at bay. Filling the thirsty rubber with my submission as I finally and utterly sink away into the blissful blank of complete surrender. I know only that every shuddering pump is a pure and freely given gift of my self to Him – a confirmation that everything I am and could ever wish to be is HIS.

––––––––

Your puppy loves you Sir, with every shred of its humanity and every drop of its puppy essence. It is PROUD to let the world know what I am:

My Master's dog, His perverted pup, His devoted rubber hound.

*"…My mouth drools as His natural musk blends with the rubber
into an amazingly heady smell of sex and masculinity…"*

"Please, Sir – I brought my sleepsack…"

I bound up the path – my tail wagging with excitement to be seeing my Man again. He opens the door with a big grin on His own face, looking resplendent in His rubber bike jacket and jeans. He is nearly knocked off His feet as I leap into His arms, barking and laughing. We reel back into the hallway as I cover His face with puppy-licks…

I finally relent when His spluttering and laughing becomes too much and He has to let me down to the floor – then I scamper along behind Him on all fours, as He leads us both into the lounge.

There, He pulls me up onto my hind legs, and wraps His arms around me in a huge enfolding embrace. He pushes my head down into His shoulder and strokes the back of my head – His deep voice vibrates in His chest as He tells me those wonderful words:

"*Good boy: I love my dog!*"

A deep sob wrenches itself from inside of me: born of my love for my Man, my surrender to Him, and the ache I feel when I am away from

Him – away from this, my true place. He rocks me gently, kisses the top of my head. He croons His love and support for His dog and tells me that He will always be here, ready with more hugs whenever I need them.

I pull my head from His shoulder, grin up at Him… But then find myself distracted by the amazingly glossy shine of His chlorinated rubber jacket – and the silky feel of it beneath my hands.

My mouth drools as His natural musk blends with the rubber into an amazingly heady smell of sex and masculinity… The beautiful eroticism of it makes my puppy-cock swell in my jeans, and I find myself start to helplessly bump my crotch against His thigh with a deep sigh. He laughs – rubs my hair – and guides my kissing mouth down along His whole rubberised body until I am on my knees again and covering the beautiful full mound of His rubber sex in doggy kisses and eagerness.

I watch and drool as He carefully unzips the rubberised fly – lets loose the meat which His dog loves and worships so deeply.

His balls hang heavy and low in a split ball-weight – He lifts His cock out of the way so that the dog can reach them with its wet muzzle, cover them with long slow licks. I circle my tongue around each ball – then gently suck each of them into the warm wet of my mouth. I find that if I suck whilst also pushing gently upwards, then I can manage to draw both balls and His entire sack into my mouth… With them held gently between my lips I am able to lick and mouth and gently tug – leaving Him sighing and grunting with pleasure – and His dog whining in excitement.

He nudges me off Him, then leads us both upstairs and into the playroom – settles the dog down onto the floor and then gives me free rein to lick and lap and tease and probe once more.

I let myself go completely to the grooming of Him – the sensation of Him against my tongue. My senses fill with the subtle differences in taste and texture over every inch of His meat: the pulsing satin smoothness of His head, the tempting wet groove of His glans, the tautness of His frenem and the sweet oozing wetness of His pre-cum…

Licking Him becomes my entire world as I am absorbed into the purely animal act of tasting and feeling. I feel myself sinking deeper into pup-space, and gratefully allow the dog-mind to rise up like a beautiful black tide to wash away all concerns and thoughts and humanity.

I lose all sense of time and identity: merge gently into becoming simply a teasing wet tongue. My efforts fed by the pleasurable groans and sighs which my attention draws from my Man.

I am lost in the pure bliss of making my Man happy.

He lets me tease Him for what might have been hours. My jaw aches and the floor between my rubbered knees is spit-slick with my drool, but I am happy and blissfully deep.

At last, I feel the swelling pulse in His head, and I know that He is close to cumming. He pulls me back by my collar – looks into my eyes and asks:

"Does my dog want feeding?"

I bark excitedly, still deep in puppy-space, and then settle back on my heels: head tipped back and tongue a red carpet of welcome for His seed…

The taste of those first drops of His cum is amazing: salt and sweet, thick and glutinous… It is too much for the dog to resist, and it hungrily swallows His meat down deep into its muzzle, down into its throat – so that it can feel Him pump His rich treasure directly into its heart.

Sated, He sinks onto His knees – then draws us both down onto the floor so that He can gather the dog bodily onto His chest. We lie there for a while whilst I feel the ragged rise and fall of His breathing settle back to restfulness.

I try to lie still, but it is not long before the sensual feel of His slick chlorinated rubber becomes too much for my dripping cock. I struggle to stop myself from gently trying to hump into His belly.

He cocks His head back, reaches up a thickly gloved hand, and lets the dog lick and suck the over-sized thumb whilst He reaches down to enfold its own meat in the other glove.

I moan around His rubbered fingers, press my face into His gloved palm – even as I helplessly hump His other tight rubber fist. I feel the rising excitement as I edge closer towards release.

It is a struggle, but I fight my way back from that edge. Before I can reach that moment of no return, I quickly beg for an indulgence:

"Please Sir – I brought my sleep-sack…"

He throws His head back and laughs:

"You pervert dog!"

But then He releases me and says:

"OK – fetch!"

He laughs even harder when I come back into the playroom on all fours – pushing the box into the room ahead of me with my nose…

He has me hop up onto the massage couch in the middle of the playroom, then helps me as I carefully ease my rubbered legs down into the tight dark confines of the sack – working my feet into the bulbous bottom. The sack is incredibly tight, and it is hard work getting my body inside it – but the struggle is eased by a generous layer of silicone lube…

I lie back as He carefully works the tight rubber up along my thighs and over my chest. At Sir's command I put my arms down inside, and obediently let Him seal them within the internal sleeves. I grunt as the tight rubber pulls them tightly against the sides of my chest.

Finally, Sir pulls the zips closed over the tops of my shoulders and up to my neck. He steps back to admire my bound and sealed body: slick and slug like within the tight rubber cocoon. Only my head remains exposed…

But then He turns to the stack of toys beside Him – and pulls out a hooded S10 gas mask…

I cannot help but grin up at Him and His knowledge of His pup's perversity. Obediently, I raise my head to let Him slide the hood over my face. I shiver as I feel the long zip pulled close around the back of my head, and the collar lock tight around my neck.

The smell of heady rubber is intoxicating as the mouthpiece settles over me. My vision of Him is blurred through the lenses, but the condensation creates a halo around His head that sparkles and shines. He smiles down wickedly at His restrained and encased dog – then He covers the lenses with two heavy rubber gloves: sealing me away into blissful darkness and the hiss and pop of the breathing ports.

I tense and release every muscle in my body, exploring the tight confines of my rubber cocoon. It does not take long to realise how effectively I am now bound – how every attempt to move is resisted and countered by the resilient rubber as it forces my encased limbs back into position, back into surrender. The effort only makes me breath harder – and the gasmask clamps itself tighter around my head.

I know that He has been letting me test the boundaries of my new rubber prison – silently watching me struggle in the blind darkness – but then I feel His hands upon me: exploring and testing my bound body for Himself. Every touch is both muffled by the multiple rubber layers and yet focused and amplified by the quiet isolation.

He moves away for a moment, and then I feel the touch of the first of His rubber floggers – gentle at first, then gradually falling heavier upon my helpless body. I strain my chest forward against the rubber, begging Him for more. I wish I were on my belly so that I could feel His pain across my eager arse.

One after another, He moves through the flogger weights, until He is finally using a beautiful heavy rubber flogger that makes me wince, groan and twitch with every impact. I am beyond pain, insulated in my rubber world and feeling each lash as the caress of His dominance and control.

I take His pain as I give Him my love: freely and with honour and Pride.

Finally, I feel Him pulling at the zipper across my crotch. His gloved hand reaches in, eases my straining cock and balls from between my thighs – releases them from the tight squeeze of the rubber. He carefully pulls the zips closed around my balls, so that the sack itself becomes a tight band around them. With my entire body so tightly and anonymously encased, my naked cock feels totally exposed and helpless.

With His gentle touch, I shudder and twitch – groan and suck hard against the breathing restriction of the hood.

His gloved fingers feel incredible as they gently stroke around my glans – causing a bead of precum to well out. He catches it in His rubbered palm, and then gently smooths it over the entire head…

I am painfully sensitive and try to pull my knees up, buck my hips away from the intensity of sensation – but He has already restrained me to the bench with chains around my bagged ankles, knees and chest, and I find these prevent me from moving at all. I can do nothing but endure – and try to writhe and moan helplessly within the mask. But even as I struggle, I find that I am also perversely thankful that His restraints make me incapable of pulling away from the awful and wonderful teasing that keeps me so painfully and tantalisingly on the edge of release – and so utterly deep in submission.

At random moments He plays with the breathing tube from the gas mask: places its open end into the warmth of His pits so that I find myself huffing and groaning with the heady scent of His masculinity. Then, without warning, He places the end over the taught rubber that covers my chest instead: so that each of my sucking breaths only succeed in pulling the tube against the air-tight rubber. With each breath, the hood clamps itself onto my gasping face like an alien creature.

The buzzing breathlessness of my asphyxia makes it feel as though the rubber squeezes tighter across my whole body – and my cock throbs harder and more eager for release…

He teases and edges me for breathless hours. Blissfully surrendered to His control, I lose all sense of self – I become only a tight rubber cock, my body shaking with the strength of my need to cum.

Only then does He finally relent. His probing fingers and stroking hands focus only on slowly pushing me over that blissfully denied edge – until I am twitching and gasping and pumping my puppy-cum over and over in laughing, howling release…

———————

He lets me free – uncovers my head and slowly unzips the resisting rubber cocoon to reveal my still-suited body. I am bathed in a pool of my own sweat…

He helps me down from the couch. We grin wickedly at each other over the ensuing careful clean up as we carefully pull each other free from our now sticky rubber.

Playroom tidy, He shuts the door and leads me along to the bedroom, where we eagerly slide into a warm dry bed.

His hand is gentle upon my collar as He guides me over to Him so that I can lay my head against His chest. I catch the scent of rubber on His skin, and give a little 'wuff' of pleasure – then I gently nuzzle His nipple between my teeth whilst I open my chest to the teasing pain His pinching fingers inflict upon my own…

He reaches over to turn out the light, then sighs as His pup scoots its warm naked body back against Him and nuzzles in under His arm. The taste of His cock is still rich in the back of my throat and the scent of His cum heady in my beard.

We lie in the dark for a while, quietly talking: recollections of the play we shared – fanning the memories into bright fire so that they will burn themselves into our memory and stay with us both forever. But it has been a long day, and so slowly we grow quieter. I nestle down deeper against Him – feel His arm come around me to hold me safe. I listen to His breathing as it slowly deepens and He falls into sleep.

I lie awake for a while, resisting the pull down into sleep. I am quietly in awe of the intense feelings of protection and comfort that lying here gives me – and relish the honour and pride that I feel at being able to sleep safe in His arms once more.

*"…I can feel my sweat trickling down underneath the
black layers, over my ribs and down my back…"*

Piss-pig

The rubber is tight and hot over my body – warmed by the sun that comes through the open sides of the summerhouse. I can feel my sweat trickling down underneath the black layers, over my ribs and down my back. I feel it dripping down into my rubber sox. It pools, and then starts to overspill and fill my waders. My sheathed cock twitches at the feeling: part sensual, part perverse…

My shoulders ache, and I pull against the chains to try to stretch them. There is just enough give to get a little relief. The movement makes the rubber slide distractingly across my skin, as the sweat drips from the rear zip of my suit and stains the wooden decking beneath my plugged arse…

Unable to find true relief, I surrender to my fate and settle back into position: rubber-encased, kneeling in my waders, arms stretched wide and exposed, the wide metal dog collar tight around my neck and padlocked to a yard-chain. I am restrained and controlled – waiting like a good dog for my Man to return…

My ears prick at the sound of His boots on the gravel path outside the summerhouse. My heart beats faster and I give an instinctive whine –

then I bark excitedly in reply to His chuckle as HE steps into the shed. Every ache and discomfort is forgotten in the wash of love that I feel at the sight of Him: my Handler, my Master, my Man.

Tall firm legs are encased in army desert camouflage fatigues, pushed into turned-down heavy-duty Century waders that match the dog's own. An olive-green T-shirt emphasises the warmth of His natural tan, and allows the thick pelt of His chest hair to show through at the neck. His pits are free, so that the dog can catch His intoxicating scent... His chest is broad, His arms strong, and His hands firm. A thick beard covers his jaw and His head is covered with neatly cropped hair. Deep green eyes stare down at His dog with a mixture of possession and ownership, passion and protective care.

He stands just out of reach, and I strain against the chains towards Him – staring up at Him with devotion and hunger and need. I try to bark and whine past the choking chain that keeps me from Him. Breathlessly, I pull against the restraint of my collar until my vision tunnels into blackness and I fear I will pass out. I can't help myself: the dog in me is too strong, and the dog needs its Man...

He takes pity on His dog, and steps closer. He lets His dog press its face into Him, bury its muzzle in His crotch. I whine and bark in pleasure as He strokes my head and says those words that mean *everything* to me:

"*Good dog!*"

I tilt my head up, tongue and muzzle still licking and nuzzling. I stare up into His eyes and let Him see the devotion and obsession, surrender and hunger that fills me – the hunger and love that makes me His dog, His pup, His boy...

Driven by that hunger, I nuzzle, lick, strain, and whine once more: trying to show Him how much the dog in me needs HIM...

"*OK boy – your Man knows what His dog wants...*"

He steps back a little. From under His brows He fixes His dog with a look of COMMAND that sends shudders of submission through me from balls to bone. He reaches down with one hand and unbuckles His thick leather belt. Slowly, He reveals His pelted stomach and the top of His bike jock. I strain hard against the collar, choke and grunt and curse the chains that keep me from lunging at Him in hunger. He laughs, and pulls the jock down – lets the dog see the head of His meat:

"*This is what my dog wants, isn't it, boy…?*"

I bark and whine, tongue panting – splattering the wooden floor with pools of drool to match the sweat that drips from my suit…

He stands there: full, thick, ready – teasing His helpless dog as it strains to reach Him, hungry only to please Him…

"*OK boy – let me see your tongue!*"

He steps closer – into range – but I know I must obey. I settle back on my heels, tilt my head back, and let my tongue loll out of my jaws: long and pink and dripping. I stare up at Him with pleading eyes.

"*Good boy! – now, lick your Man's balls*"

I go to work: long, slow licks, just as He has taught me. I encircle each of His balls with my tongue, coating them in dog-drool, letting my beard and moustache graze the side of His meat – massaging each meaty globe and feeling them writhe and squirm as I work up His juices. I let myself become utterly absorbed, totally lost in the task. The smell and the taste of Him takes me down further, deeper into pup-space, more purely and perfectly a dog – HIS dog.

"*Gooood boy!*"

He croons, and I feel shudders of pleasure at His encouragement – and the pride of knowing I am making my Man happy.

He rests His hands on my shoulders, and I know that it is time. I pull back from my licking, tip my face back with my tongue out and my mouth relaxed: waiting, obedient, ready…

I feel Him give my head a stroke as reward – then slowly, teasingly, His meat upon my tongue. Everything in me wants to lick and suck, but I know I must control myself – do only as I am told. So I kneel where I am, keep my head still – wait…

"OK, dog – take your Man's piss"

It comes slowly at first – trickles into me, hot and salty – then suddenly it is a steady pungent stream. I struggle to gulp down every golden drop like a good dog. My dog-cock drips and strains in my sheath and a moan escapes from deep inside me as I drink down His piss and feel it filling me, changing me.

"You fuckin pervert!" I hear Him croon, *"my perverted fuckin dog!"*

The golden flow slows, and then stops. He pulls out.

I know He's not finished and wonder why… Then He pushes my head down, bares the zipped neck of my suit. I feel my dog-collar tighten as He grabs it, pushes His still hard cock down inside. His hands are powerful on my shoulders as He holds me there: submissive and kneeling beneath Him, staring at the toes of His waders… Then all I can think of is the wash of His piss as it flows down inside my rubber – over my back and shoulders, filling up my suit just as He has already filled my throat. The pure perverted pleasure of it makes me squirm and grunt: hot man-piss sluicing down, pooling around my plugged arse, washing down my legs and filling my waders, bubbling out of my arse zip and dripping from my sheath…

"Yeah – filling up my dog's rubber – my urinal-suited piss-pup…"

He empties His bladder into me, and then lets me go. I sink back to my haunches, lost in the perverted pleasure of being bathed in His piss… He knows that this has been a long held fantasy of mine – to stew in my man's juices, to take my Man whilst I am filled with His piss inside and out – and now He has gifted me with the perverted reality.

I kneel in a spreading pool of yellow. I know that He can clearly see my wet straining sheath: the pure animal response to His marking. I know that He understands this piggish reaction at being so rewarded, so perverted…

He ruffles my piss-wet hair:

"*That's it: my piggy little pervert pup!*"

I squirm in the wet rubber, kneeling at His feet. I pant and drool and grin back up at Him – hoping and knowing what will come next.

I buzz with perversity and Pride – happy and hungry to be His: His pup, His dog, His pig. His whole damned barn-yard if He wants it, just so long as I'm HIS…

"…and He always has me wear my full rubber dog-suit, dog-hood and tail-plug when He takes me out to a club…"

A night encased

I love rubber.

The feel of it tight against the skin: containing, restraining, defining. It is an intoxicating and erotic experience. But although I have regularly worn rubber for long periods, I have never yet had the chance to spend a night fully encased – to sleep in rubber.

At least, not until the last visit with my Handler…

————

My Handler always likes His dog to be in some form of rubber. He even has me wear some beneath my clothes when I am leathered and ready to pillion for Him on His bike, or trotting beside Him in 'civvies' whilst out in town. Sometimes it is only a jock, or shorts – but often it is sleeveless long-johns, or a full one-piece catsuit – and He *always* has me wear my full rubber dog-suit, dog-hood and tail-plug when He takes me out to a club. He knows from experience that I will be kept horny and focused by that feeling of tight rubber enfolding my body.

This last visit Master had me wear my neck-entry sleeveless suit from Invincible, made for me in 0.5mm grade glossy black rubber: super tight and stretchy and silicone lubed. Every movement made the latex stretch and slide across my body, and pulled against my crotch – constantly reminding me of my sex and its encasement. My cock teased and squeezed by a neoprene cock-ring under the rubber and a plug rubbing up into my fuck-hole, to keep it – and the dog within me – hungry and ready.

I had then covered all of that tight rubber beneath the multiple layers of my leather uniform shirt, jeans, chaps and boots: turning my body into a tightly wrapped leather-boy package for my Master to slowly strip – gradually exposing the rubber-pervert hiding within…

It was a fantastic day of horny play, and by the time my Master was dragging His dog up to bed, I had already spent nearly 15 hours in that rubber skin. Normally I would be uncomfortable after wearing the rubber for so long – but the thin rubber is so flexible, and the suit is so beautifully made, that it really felt too good to want to take off. It felt so much a part of my skin and k9 identity that I would have felt truly naked without it. And so the dog's Master let His rubber pervert-pup curl up next to Him under the duvet. My body hot against Him in my rubber skin: a super-heated rubber-dog hot-water bottle to keep my Man warm all night. Contented, I gently nuzzled into His enfolding arms and bumped my rubbered and plugged tail against His thigh. I quietly whined when He reached a hand over me, so that He could stroke the rubber, tight across my crotch: rubbing and teasing the cock safely trapped inside….

I thought that I would not be able to sleep – that the encasement would keep me too aroused, or that the rubber would become too hot and uncomfortable. But I always feel so safe curled up with my Man – enfolded, protected, restrained by my Master's arms and His Masculinity – and soon I found myself relaxing, despite my arousal. It felt so good to lie there, warmed by the heat of His body through my rubber – His breath soft and calming on my collared neck, and the rise and fall of His chest against my back – and I soon found my mind drifting to His gently crooning words as He soothed His dog down into submission and sleep.

I felt so happy and content, and before I knew it, I could feel my body relax and my mind drift into that perfect non-thinking puppy space – and down deep into sleep and dreams…

———

It was an incredible feeling to slowly wake the next morning – still enfolded within my rubber after more than 24 hours…

Slowly, I drifted up from the depths of an intense doggy dream, and into the intoxicating smell of my hot rubbered body and my Master's musk. My awareness slowly growing around the feel of my Master's hand stroking the trapped curve of my cock through the suit – His body encircling my own and gently grinding the plug into my aching hole with His weight…

My dog's body awoke before my mind did – woke into arousal and pup-identity – and into the reality of my still-rubbered flesh and my eager need to please and serve…

I rolled over onto my glossy belly: exposing my tightly rubbered arse to my Master's stroking touch. I felt cool air as the zipper was pulled open, dimly aware of the hungry noises I made into the pillow as my hole surrendered the plug to the tug of my Master's strong hands. Without thought, my body responded to His quiet command of *"Give…"*

And then, His voice breathed into my ear: *"Open up for me, boy… gently now – let me in…"*

Still sleepy – my awareness slowly dawning – I resisted that pull into consciousness so that I might stay enfolded in the bliss of simply being His pup – of giving myself to Him for His pleasure. Automatically, I curved my hole up to meet Him – relaxing and opening – letting Him take His dog.

I felt His power and passion build, and built with it – without thought or limitation. Knowing my submission only makes Him take control – driving Him deeper, harder. The Master within Him awoken by the dog inside me.

I felt Him take my wrists then, as He pushed me down with His weight. My body wriggling and writhing under Him in rubber-submission – my legs pinned beneath His, my hands held in His fists – panting and whining in response to His growls as He fucked His rubber-dog and took His pleasure from its greedy perversion…

Man and dog, Master and hound. Fucking His dog, breeding His pup – making it whole…

"…I think about the time in the sling-room at 'The Web' in Amsterdam: my waders up in the stirrups, arms grabbing the chains above my head…"

Fuck-pup

I am a horny dog with a hungry hole – thinking about my Man. Thinking about Him and being fucked by Him. Feeling that need deep inside me: the need to submit, the need to open and give myself to Him…

I pull on my rubber and work with a plug. I let my mind fill with thoughts of my Master as I train my hole to take more – *want* more.

I whimper and whine as I remember the feeling of being open to HIM, of submitting my hole to HIM – of being filled and completed and fucked by HIM: down into submission, down into pup-space, down into being His dog…

As I play with my hole, I let my mind fill with memories of Him – and of all the times that He has fucked me and made me feel whole…

I remember the dog's first time: timid but eager to please – lying back in my Master's sling. My Master between my legs, gently teasing and training my virgin hole with His lubed fingers – kissing my thighs and belly and telling me to relax. His gloved hands gently stroking my body and teasing my cock. Hearing His crooning, encouraging words when I whimpered or whined from the onslaught… keeping my mind distracted with a strap around my balls and clamps on my nips – both linked to a weighted chain that hung from the ceiling, and that He set to swinging whenever I found His intrusion too much.

My Man gently teaching my doggy-mind to trust Him as my body learnt to take the pleasure and the pain, to submit and *'Open up for Me, boy…'*

I think about our later training sessions: my body strapped down to His fuck-bench, my head in a gasmask and my feet in boots – pinned on my back with my legs pressed hard to my chest. My Master driving deep and hard into my dog-hole as I groan and bark and pant within the respirator – struggling to take Him, *Wanting* to take Him. PROUD to please Him…

I think about the time in the sling-room at 'The Web' in Amsterdam: my waders up in the stirrups, arms grabbing the chains above my head – staring up at the mirror on the ceiling and seeing my body stretched out and panting in hunger: my Man beautiful and powerful above me as He fucked me so hard that we nearly brought the ceiling down…

And I think about lying beside and beneath Him in His bed at night: my body safely wrapped in His tight arms as He gently fucks His pup down into sleep.

––––––––

All these thoughts swim and pulse in my doggy-head – as my hole twitches and burns around the plug and my heart aches. All I want, all I *need* is my Man and His meat – His pleasure and my own surrender…

I train my hole, and know I am His dog: train hard for Him, and wish that I was with my Man so I could give Him my hole, my body and my everything…

"… His leathered crotch pressed against the tank, feeling the throb of the engine and remembering how it felt to be fucking His pup…"

Rubber rider

The petrol tank feels cool against my cheek – and through the thin rubber skin stretched tight across my sweating chest and stomach. I can see my breath mist against the metal as I pant and struggle and writhe: frantic and lost in intense pleasure. I place my gloved hands on the handlebars, push my booted feet onto the foot-rests: rear my rubbered haunches up, to press myself back hard against my Man – and catch sight of us both where we are reflected in the wing-mirrors…

I am encased in tightly revealing full black rubber: high-necked one-piece suit and gloves, thick rubber sheath and codpiece – even my feet are encased in tight rubber sox within the knee-high rubber-riding boots that cover my legs.

The tight glossy rubber makes me feel closely contained and utterly controlled – yet it also defines and exposes every twitching muscle, every bulging ache of my arousal. The only visible shreds of my humanity are the black-ringed eyes that stare from within the moulded rubber hood that reshapes my head into that of a dog – and the hot ring of my twitching hole. But even that is now hidden: pressed back against the furred belly of my Master so that He can fill my rubbered core with His heat and His hunger.

My glossy black encased body is laid across the silver tank of His 1300cc super-bike – hugged against the tank and pinioned beneath Him so that I am pressed down hard into the broad leather saddle. With my body hugged tight around the idling machine, my arse is raised high and my hole forced open – filled with HIM – as tight and hungry as the pistons that throb and pulse within the engine beneath us.

This is His bike – His steed – and He rides me now as He has ridden it: with unquestioned ease and complete control. Every deep thrust rocks the bike rhythmically forward on its centre stand – and pushes my wrapped and packaged crotch painfully deeper into the leather seat. His gloved hand grasps my neck – just above the padlocked silver collar that marks me as His property – forces me back down to the tank and pins my head against the cool metal. In the heat and the hunger I have a mind-twisting vision that my rubbered flesh is somehow merging to the metal and leather and chrome of His bike – and my sheathed cock throbs all the closer to an untouched orgasm at my desire for such total surrender into becoming nothing more than another of His treasured possessions…

He thrusts Himself deep into me and I feel the press of His thickly furred balls against my hole. I moan, try to turn my head against the press of His hand – and leave a thin slick trail of saliva against the cool metal.

He relents: moves His hands and takes a hold of my waist instead – holding me powerless in His grasp as He pulls me up and back against Him. In response, I clench and tense my deep inner ring of muscle – feel the hot thickness of Him squeezed within me – and hear His explosive gasp of pleasure in return.

He releases my waist – lets me rock forwards on the foot-rests, taking control as I slide my hole forwards and back along His sheathed length – clenching and relaxing as I do so. I can't help grinning at His reflected look of pleasure in the mirror before I close my eyes and give myself over to the intensity of this hunger He seeds within me.

For a moment, I am lost in the feeling of Him inside me – in the pleasure of this fullness, this complete surrender. My body instinctively responds to His intrusion without thought: gently rocks back and forth in a luxurious curve that slides Him along the entire inner bulge of my prostate. I shudder as the ridge of His glans tweaks the outer ring of my inner muscle on His outward stroke, then gasp as He pushes upwards and forwards into the silky folds of my core. He lies back against the pillion seat – surrendered in turn to the intensity of feeling that His pup's tight hole gives Him. His eyes half close in the sensuality of being served – and I feel a wash of pure puppyish joy at being able to give Him such pleasure…

––––––––––

Intense and perfect though this moment is, I am in awe that it is only the end of a perfect day-long session with my Master. A full day within my rubber, serving Him with my body in so many ways: plugged and humping on His boot – bathing Him in my spit and giving Him my throat – lying piniored on the fuck-bench beneath Him, His cock so deep within my throat that all breath and thought were impossible: held in stillness and waiting for His permission to start again… of being strapped down and fucked deep: legs folded and restrained hard up against my chest as He drilled His hunger down into me and took possession of my soul with His hungry gaze.

I begged Him to strap me down into the rubber cocoon of my sleep-sack then – to convert me into nothing more than a rubberised fuck-toy: a double-ended rubber slug of hunger to feed upon His juices. But He refused – preferring instead to bring us down here into the garage: onto the bike, this silver steed – His most loved possession and symbol to me of His power.

To act out this long held fantasy of us both. To have my trembling rubber body up on the pegs, over the saddle. To fuck me, ride me, and make me a part of His machine.

————

All of this flickers through my mind as my body twists and grinds upon Him: perverted fuel for the arousal that builds and burns within the enclosing rubber – oozing from my collar and cuffs and dripping from the edges of my zippered hole…

He lies back and lets me slowly fuck myself against Him: revels in the feeling of being so deep within the willing core of His perverted rubber pup. I catch His eye in the mirror as He watches the lights glisten and ripple from my glossy skin – and feel myself transformed in the possession I see in His gaze.

I am dog, I am rubber, I am hunger – and I am HIS.

He finally pushes me back against the tank when He feels me rising towards my own puppyish orgasm – ignores my whimpers as He slowly draws Himself out from me. I struggle and clench, wanting to feel Him still there inside of me – until He has to command me to relax so that He can pull Himself free from the clinging hold of my despairing ring.

He swings his tall booted leg across and over me – dismounts the bike and His hound. He moves to stand beside it, leather encased legs square upon the cool concrete of the garage floor – His meat now straining and ready in His gloved hand.

He gives the order, and I obediently sink to my knees before Him – my hands balled and pressed into the floor like the paws they have now become.

He stares down at His dog with possessive hunger. I know that my service has brought Him close to cumming, and so I raise my hooded muzzle towards Him: open and willing, my tongue hot, wet, pink, and ready.

His hand is gentle upon my head as He holds me perfectly still – and His voice is thick with encouragement as I greedily and gratefully receive the gift of His seed.

————

As we leave the garage – just before He turns out the light – I see Him look back at the chrome and steel of His mechanical steed. I know that he will be thinking of His dog and its hole when He is next out riding: His leathered crotch pressed against the tank, feeling the throb of the engine and remembering how it felt to be fucking His pup – and His machine through it…

When He finally sends me home, I have still not cum – nor do I need to: serving Him has given me more pleasure than any orgasm ever could.

"…It's amazing what you can do and where you can
go if you put on a high-vis and a hard-hat…"

Waders and high-vis

Sir took His pup for a surprise trip down to the coast at the last Bank Holiday.

I knew that there was something interesting a-foot when He sent me strict and explicit instructions to bring my full rubber, my waders and a high-vis waistcoat… I'll let Him describe just what it was that He had planned:

"The weather was due to be wet, and I knew we had a lot of gear to carry, so I decided we would go down in the car. I normally prefer to go by bike, but my pup kept me talking and laughing all the way, and so the journey went quickly…

I got us checked in to our sea-front hotel as soon as we got to the coast, then led my pup out to stand on the beach. The wind was a little cold, so he pushed up against me to nestle under my arm as we took a long look at the rolling breakers and the long spit of the pier, dark against the skyline…

After a while, I pushed him away and suggested that we take the rest of our bags to the room and then "go for a walk on the sand" – to which the pup grinned and barked his ascent.

Back in the room, My dog guessed what was really going on when I told him to get into his rubber one-piece, waders and high-viz. – whilst I pulled on my own heavy rubber suit and jacket. When we were both fully geared, I then handed him his own yellow hard-hat and walked us back out though the hotel and onto the beach.

It felt good to be stomping down the shingle and walking out to the water's edge: the rubber warm and tight and our waders heavy. I saw a few people give us startled looks, but the pup could not keep the grin of his face or hide the bulge in his rubber.

I had timed our arrival with low tide, so we had quite a walk down to the sea's edge. The sea and sky were amazing, and I had the dog take some pictures of us before we clomped along the tide line – watching the seaweed swaying in the current as the tide started to turn and the water began to rush back up the beach. All that cold flowing water made me need to piss – and the dog took a photo as my piss arced out into the sea…

We stomped along through rapidly filling rock-pools and finally made our way to the pier itself.

It was a beautifully imposing Victorian structure, and it was amazing to see all the ironwork from so close – so I led my pup underneath, to see how the legs and struts were covered with debris and barnacles and muscles – and dozens of small-holed pebbles that had become threaded with discarded fishing-line and tangled around each strut by the tide. I also had great fun watching my dog hunting for small fish, crabs, and anemones in the various pools – and spotting worm casts and the indentations where razor fish had been.

A couple of times I noticed the people on the pier above us – looking down and stopping in surprise to see what they thought were workmen at work so late in the day. It's amazing what you can do and where you can go if you put on a high-vis and a hard-hat.

It felt very special to be sharing that transient place between tides with my dog, and we stopped for quite a while to take several pictures: amongst the metalwork in our wet rubber and heavy boots, and framing the evening sky and sea beneath the decking of the pier. It was both beautiful and perverse: nature in the raw and rubber at its most basic and protective.

Photos done, I then led us back out from under the metalwork – past a storm drain outfall as we stomped our way back up the beach. I couldn't help but chuckle as an entire family of four stood motionless and spellbound as we appeared from underneath the pier: no doubt amazed to see two men in wet shining rubber.

As we walked back up the beach, my dog found a special pebble with two holes in it. It was his little 'good luck' gift to me, and it now sits on the ledge above my desk as a reminder of our special time together…

———

By now, it was getting late, and I was hungry – so I led us up off the beach and into town, looking for food. We finally ordered chips and onion rings from one of the sea-front chip-shops: both of us still in rubber, hi-viz. and waders and my pup snuggled back into me whilst I wrapped my arms around him to keep him warm. I knew that we were probably scaring the bemused onlookers, but I honestly couldn't give a damn because I was with my dog and I am proud of how freely and openly he shows his love and devotion to me.

A bag of warm chips in our hands, I led us back to the shore: through a Bank Holiday funfair as the workmen dismantled it, ready to move on. Both of us grinned as we walked past the dodgems: the electric sparks flying to the fading sounds of 'Dancing Queen' over the sound-system.

Back on the beach I found us a little 'table' amongst the sea-eroded groins, and then quietly hand-fed my dog with chips and onion rings – until I accidentally knocked over our bottle of drink and covered him in sticky lemonade…

As we ate and laughed, the sun slowly set and the illuminations came up on the pier; both fiery sun and shining lights reflecting in the now returned tide. I had my dog turn so that he could sit directly in front of me to watch, craning his neck to see where we had stood under the pier, now entirely covered by the sea. With my arms strong and protective around his rubber body, we talked about our adventure on the shore.

With the sun set and the night cooling, I finally led us back along the beach towards the hotel – the reflective panels on our high-vis catching the fairground light in the increasing darkness.

But now I didn't *want* us to be noticed, and so it was time to remove our jackets and go into stealth mode as I led My dog under the old bandstand: exploring a new iron structure of vertical pillars and diagonal struts in the half-light. The ceiling grew lower and lower as we crunched up the tide-driven shingle, and I was glad that I was wearing my hard hat when I banged my head on the low beams hidden in the dark.

At the top of the shingle I turned back – looked out from the darkness at the 200-degree view. The surf glowed ghostly as it crashed along the tide-line, and the beach bisected by the dark slashes of the groins as far as the eye could see – noting how the sea-front lamps caught and glittered upon the rocks and the waves. As I looked out at the simple beauty of it, I was also quietly taking stock of the blackness that enveloped us here within the forest of rusting supports: checking that we were now effectively invisible in the damp darkness…

Sure that we would be unseen, I relieved my dog of his backpack. I pulled out long industrial rubber gloves for the both of us: a signal to him of the start of perverted play. His silent obedience was beautiful as he fell to his wadered knees, tongue already hanging from his eager mouth.

The sensation of that wet doggy tongue on my smooth rubber was amazing as he licked and lapped at the bitter rubber – making it slick and slippery, and stimulating the Man beneath.

I let him lick and nuzzle for a while, then carefully unzipped my suit and let the dog take his reward: already semi hard and smelling of heady rubber and piss and Man. It felt so good to have my dog huff the mixed aromas deep into his body – then gently take its Man into his muzzle so that I could feel the blissful union of both Man and dog. I basked in the feeling of his quiet bark around my cock – his instinctive response to my gently spoken "Good boy", uttered as a murmur in the silent darkness.

I felt my dog's tongue hot and wet on the dorsum of my cock. I could feel his heavy rubber sheathed 'paws' holding the back of my legs, and knew that he could feel the cool smoothness of my own gloved hand on the back of his collared neck.

He could breathe at first, but as my cock swelled, I could feel it fill his airway and his breathing became mine: at my mercy and under my control as my cock engulfed his throat.

Reluctantly, I finally had to release him. I allowed him five breaths, and then the controlling plug was replaced. His tongue flickered around my cock. I relished the extra stimulation, and knew that the dog could feel his Man's buck in response. He is a good dog and I could feel his perverted mind yielding slowly to his Man's control.

I held him there, gagged, until I could feel him struggle for air, and then released him to breathe. He gasped in the sea air, but after five quick breaths, I plugged his throat once more. He is an obedient dog, and did not resist me – and I rewarded him with a low muttered "Good dog" that had him wriggling his puppy-butt in pleasure.

I kept him there like that: breathing when I allowed him, filling and gagging him when I desired. His obedience and service was perfect – and deeply satisfying.

I felt his paws stroke under my balls, then stroke along my perineum: his gloved fingers finding the heat of my puckered hole and pressing against it. His attention stirred my hunger all the more: I reached into the pocket of my rubber jacket and pulled out the bottle of lube I had saved for his own hole – reached down to grab his gloved wrist and pulled his hand up to me. I could sense his confusion as the cool lube spread over his fingers and hand, then his understanding as I guided him back to my hole and told him "Good boy – it's OK: please your Man".

His fingers gently stroked and probed – making sure that he had understood what I was ordering him to do – then they gained in confidence and certainty as he felt my cock pulse even harder in his throat in response. I let myself become absorbed in the feeling of my pup's fingers, teasing and pushing into me. They stroked around in lazy circles that matched the curl of his tongue around my cock head – then slowly slid in and out in time to his bobbing head as he thrust my cock deep into his throat. That incredible feeling was so intense and fantastic that it soon pushed me to the point where I *had* to fuck him at last.

I quietly told him to stand, then grabbed his neck with my gloved hand and pushed him backwards – holding him captive against the crossed ironwork of the pier that surrounded us. His face was eerie and pale in the darkness, and his eyes deep and black with arousal. I pulled him to me then, and forced my tongue into his mouth. I could taste my own precum where it coated his tongue and lubricated his throat.

I grabbed his hands, twisted him around so that his chest was pressed against the metal. He grunted, as his rubbered crotch was ground against the struts. He tried to turn his head as I reached down to pull the zipper of his suit, his hips pushing backwards in hunger – then he hung his head in surrender as he felt my gloves slowly ease out the plug that had kept his hole sealed and safe for me: Mine and *only* Mine to use.

Cool lube coated my hand as I pushed my heavily rubbered fingers into his hole. I felt the heat inside him, and knew that he must have felt the same when he pushed his own fingers into me. I had my revenge then, as I probed and teased his hole, and could feel him trying to relax and open up to my command – felt his struggle to give me his hole just as he had given me his throat.

I stood and looked down with hunger at his rubber body, shining in the half-light as I slowly eased the rubber-sheath over my straining cock – his arms braced against the iron struts for purchase as his butt arched back towards me in invitation and surrender. His hole was hot and wet around my head as I slowly but mercilessly pushed myself into him, inch by inch – feeling for his muscles to clench and then relax. My dog opening up to his Man – to his Meat.

I felt his body tremble when I finally thrust myself fully into him – heard his carefully bitten-back whimper. I knew that he was having to strain to take my full length and size, but it is his hunger to please me, despite his own discomfort, that makes him such a good dog to play with. I let him catch his breath – let his muscles relax and get used to my invasion – then slowly started to grind myself down into him, harder, faster, deeper… letting myself take full control of his body. Taking my pleasure from him and from his fully willing surrender.

As I fucked him harder, I could hear the squeak of our waders where they touched – and feel the slap of my balls against the tight rubber of his thighs. The feeling was intoxicating.

I fucked him hard – driven mad by the rippling clench of his muscles as he worked my cock with his hole like he has been trained to do. My hands grabbed his waist and pulled him back against me until I could feel the tight inner ring of his hole spasm tightly around the head of my cock, milking me ever closer to the shuddering orgasm I knew would come. The intensity of my attack on his core made him growl and grunt in animal hunger. As I fucked him harder, reaching for my own release, these instinctive animal sounds only got louder. I gagged him with a gloved hand over his mouth, but as I pushed deep into him at the point of cumming he finally let out a long hungry howl that echoed back to us from the surf and the ironwork around us…

I guess it was finally too much, because there was the sound of questioning voices from the decking above us – and the sound of feet crossing the boards and down onto the beach…

I made him stand still and silent whilst I watched someone come to peer under the structure – glad that I had made us both remove our high-vis, and knowing that we would remain invisible so long as we stayed still and quiet. Finally the figure moved away – but it was too close a call. Once I was sure they had gone, I had the dog zip himself up, then carefully and silently led us back out onto the beach.

––––––––––

It was a breathless Man and dog that finally slipped back to our hotel room: falling onto the bed, grinning and laughing – my pup lying sprawled upon my chest.

I pulled him around so that he was nestled between my legs. As I did so, I could feel his dog-cock, hard and wet inside the prison of its rubber. He gave a little whine and a helpless little hump – and I knew that his doggy-brain was eager to be allowed to cum too…

I toyed with the idea of getting him to sit on my cock, but realised that his hole would be sore after the abuse I had just given it. I couldn't face his disappointment if he wasn't able take me – and wasn't sure that *I* had the strength to cum again so soon… So I stroked his head and smiled up into his face – and gave him permission to bring himself off against me: telling him to hump my thigh like the true puppy that he really is.

He grinned, then gave a proper little doggy 'wuff' as he buried his head into the rubber over my chest – his doggy butt wagging as his hips bumped against my thigh. I could feel his cock moving against me, slick and wet within his rubber – hear his animal whines as he lost himself in pure and overwhelming puppy-sensations. And then I could feel the spreading heat of his cum as he finally pushed himself over the edge and filled his rubber with a shuddering howl…

I let us both snuggle for a while in the warmth, wrapped in the heady scent of hot, wet rubber and post-cum dog. I traced my hand across his body, made him squirm by stroking the rubber over his now sensitive cock head. I could feel his trapped cum as it squelched under the thin rubber skin that kept it and his cock sealed and insulated – the rubber that makes him my perfect little pup and devoted pervert.

I toyed with the idea of making him sleep in that rubber, knowing that it would keep him in this horny and obedient state – but I was tired and knew we had an early morning check-out, and so I had to relent and send him scampering for the shower to peel off his layers and get ready for bed.

————

Despite my best intentions, we were both tired and heady in the morning.

It was a rough and difficult drive home, but I made a stop at a hillside-cafe on the way – using the excuse to show the dog the view over the city and the docks. The clean air and hot tea made me feel better – but really it was my dog's loving company and the memory of his surrender that made the drive back so much fun.

I love my dog. He is a horny and deeply perverted pup.

He is all and only Mine, and I know that he loves and obeys Me without question.

What Master could ever wish for more."

"…But that's just me – a confirmed pervert. Join us – what do you have to lose? Besides, perhaps, your sanity…"

A rubber postscript

OK, so I admit it: I am just a little obsessed with fetish and rubber.

Over the years, I have tried to explain to others why rubber drives me into such perversity – and why rubber features so highly in both my erotic identity, and my stories. But the trouble is, unless you have worn rubber – felt the way it stretches and conforms to your body and ripples over your skin – then it is a little hard to understand just how intoxicatingly erotic a material it is to wear…

You see, rubber is like an insulator: it reflects back your own sexual power, arousal, and perversity – holds it inside of you and amplifies it even more. That building heat and arousal easily overwhelms you, and turns you into sex itself…

Rubber holds in your own heat, slicks your skin with sweat and lube, and translates each touch or movement into overpowering sensation…

Rubber has very low thermal properties, so whilst it bathes you in your own sweat it also makes you incredibly aware of the cold air that whispers over your body – or the *heat* of your partner's touch…

When you wear rubber clothing that is tight and body conforming, you can feel it exerting an irresistible pressure across your entire skin – feel it squeezing and caressing you within its inescapable encasement… Skin-tight, rubber also reveals every bump and indentation, every line of muscle and tendon. Within its black sheen it exposes and highlights every movement of your body beneath the glossy skin: every sensitively raised nipple, every bulge and twitch of your trapped cock.

It leaves you feeling completely exposed, even whilst you are fully encased.

Rubber also transforms the body within the industrialised embrace of its glossy black, waterproofing skin. Its smooth anonymity removes all individuality, and turns you into a faceless entity. In doing so it seeps into your psyche and slowly changes you into its own image…

Even the act of putting on rubber can be an intensely erotic experience. The way you must struggle and slide into it, inch by careful inch, forcing your will upon the fabric… But then you realise that, difficult though it may be to put on, it is even harder to take off – that the rubber is in fact crawling up your body and slowly eating you away…

Wearing full rubber can drive this perverted little worm almost insane with frustrated arousal. It robs it of all outer identity, seals it away from reality. It worms into its head, and eats away all self-control. It is like a black demon that infests and possesses me – takes over my mind and makes me incapable of anything except drooling, dripping, submission and perversity…

I pull on the rubber, lock on the collar, and I can *feel* the rubber eat away at me – making me its own…

The first time I wore rubber I was in my late teens – I was still living at home, still in the closet and very fucked up. I finally gave in to my urges and bravely went into a sex shop in Soho where I bought a pair of leggings, a long T-shirt, and a hood – and then sneakily tried it all on one evening when my parents were out. Just the feel of the rubber had me hard and breathless - and I just got more aroused as I struggled to pull each layer on – panicking when I got my arms stuck at one point, imagining myself unable to get it back off again, and being found out as a pervert when the family got back...

Then, finally, I turned to look at my mirrored reflection in the full-length mirror. I felt an explosive pulse of shock and arousal to see my body swallowed up in all that blackness – transformed from a nervous skinny little gay-boy into something inhuman and strangely powerful... With shaking hands I held up the hood, then watched my reflected self as I slid it over my head. Breathless, I watched the rubber ripple over my face – slicking over the last shreds of my guilty identity and replacing it with pure black anonymity...

A black-skinned, anonymous being stared back at me from the mirror. There was no sign of me – no sign of the scared young man, confused and guilty over his desires – only this glossy being of pure sex and hungry desire whose shiny waterproof skin enclosed and devoured my own.

When I reached down to touch myself, my touch was met only by the yielding warmth of the latex: slick and inhuman and seemingly burning with desire. But I could still feel my body move: encased and defined by the tight blackness. I could still see the line of my muscles as they tensed, the hard nub of my raised nipples – and the twitching line of my cock, trapped against my belly.

Every movement seemed amplified by the clinging restriction. I bent forward, moved my hips, stretched my arms – and felt the rubber skin move with me, resist me, define me... But as I moved and got more aroused, so I also started to sweat – felt it slide down beneath the rubber, pooling within its waterproofing layers. The smooth inner layers of rubber soaked up the heat – transforming it into a slick layer of lubrication until it was flowing freely against me: wet and erotic and tingling against my skin.

As I moved and sweated and shivered in excitement I felt that I was slowly being dissolved in the heat and the sweat – and this rubber-skinned being's desire…

In the dark clinging perfection and arousal, I found myself writhing and gasping. My hands fumbled across my newly alien body: stroking, pinching, grabbing and slapping at the rubbery resistance. Finally, they found the slick bulge of my crotch, and the sensations that shot through me were electric. I found myself down on my knees and then on all fours – arching and curling my back and thrusting my hips – my rubber imprisoned cock trapped against my abs and slicked with precum: fucking my own body and the rubber that encased me…

When I finally came, it was the most intense and pleasurable experience I had ever had. From that moment, I was hooked – and all I wanted was to feel that seductive power over and over again.

So you see, *that* is why I am now so obsessed with rubber. Call it a formative experience – or perhaps just the early stages of perversity. Whatever it was, the rubber had me in its siren-power.

True, it may sometimes border on obsession – but this rubber fetish is just too delicious and perverse: and I embrace it completely.

But that's just me – a confirmed pervert. You really *do* have to try it yourself to know. So go on, don't be shy: buy yourself some rubber, try it on. Be seduced by its glossy transformation and erotic control.

Join us.

What do you have to lose?

Besides, perhaps, your sanity…

About the Author

bootbrush: 'A Man's best friend is His dog...'

bootbrush has been an active member of the fetish and pup-play communities for over 15 years. A devoted pup and a committed pervert, he can regularly be found at His Handler's side – on all fours, collared and grinning – at BDSM events and fetish clubs throughout the UK and Europe.

bootbrush has always had a love for writing – and has shared both his experiences and his fiction through community forums and his own website since the earliest days of the 'net. His experiences have taught him that BDSM and pup-play can be a positive and transformative experience – for both Master *and* sub. His writing explores this, and his stories often feature a deeply hypnotic style that enables the reader to share in the intense emotional and physical release that is possible through this kind of play. This is the first time his stories have appeared in print.

bootbrush lives in the UK, where he shares his life and devotion with both his partner of 20 years and his Handler of 6. He is currently working on a new book for the 'Woof' pup-play series, published by Nazca Plains.

.

www.ingramcontent.com/pod-product-compliance
Lightning Source LLC
Chambersburg PA
CBHW051827020726
47502CB00005B/1668